# CAPTIVE OF FATE

## Zapf Chancery Tertiary Level Publications

*A Guide to Academic Writing* by C. B. Peter (1994)
*Africa in the 21st Century* by Eric M. Aseka (1996)
*Women in Development* by Egara Kabaji (1997)
*Introducing Social Science: A Guidebook* by J. H. van Doorne (2000)
*Elementary Statistics* by J. H. van Doorne (2001)
*Iteso Survival Rites on the Birth of Twins* by Festus B. Omusolo (2001)
*The Church in the New Millennium: Three Studies in the Acts of the Apostles* by
  John Stott (2002)
*Introduction to Philosophy in an African Perspective* by Cletus N.Chukwu
  (2002)
*Participatory Monitoring and Evaluation* by Francis W. Mulwa and Simon
  N. Nguluu (2003)
*Applied Ethics and HIV/AIDS in Africa* by Cletus N. Chukwu (2003)
*For God and Humanity: 100 Years of St. Paul's United Theological
  College* Edited by Emily Onyango (2003)
*Establishing and Managing School Libraries and Resource Centres* by
  Margaret Makenzi and Raymond Ongus (2003)
*Introduction to the Study of Religion* by Nehemiah Nyaundi (2003)
*A Guest in God's World: Memories of Madagasca*r by Patricia McGregor
  (2004)
*Introduction to Critical Thinking* by J. Kahiga Kiruki (2004)
*Theological Education in Contemporary Africa* edited by
  GrantLeMarquand and Joseph D. Galgalo  (2004)
*Looking Religion in the Eye* edited by Kennedy Onkware (2004)
*Computer Programming: Theory and Practice* by Gerald Injendi (2005)
*Demystifying Participatory Development* by Francis W. Mulwa (2005)
*Music Education in Kenya: A Historical Perspective* by Hellen A. Odwar
  (2005)
*Into the Sunshine: Integrating HIV/AIDS into Ethics Curriculum* Edited
  by Charles Klagba and C. B. Peter (2005)
*Integrating HIV/AIDS into Ethics Curriculum: Suggested Modules* Edited
  by Charles Klagba (2005)
*Dying Voice (An Anthropological Novel)* by Andrew K. Tanui (2006)
*Participatory Learning and Action (PLA): A Guide to Best Practice* by
  Enoch Harun Opuka (2006)
*Science and Human Values: Essays in Science, Religion, and Modern Ethical Issues*
  edited by Nehemiah Nyaundi and Kennedy Onkware (2006)
*Understanding Adolescent Behaviour* by Daniel Kasomo (2006)
*Students' Handbook for Guidance and Counselling* by Daniel Kasomo (2007)
*BusinessOrganization an Management: Questions and Answers* by Musa O. Nyakora
  (2007)
*Auditing Priniples: A Stuents' Handbook* by Musa O. Nyakora (2007)
*The Concept of Botho and HIV/AIDS in Botswana* edite by Joseph B. R. Gaie and
  Sana K. MMolai (2007)
*Captive of Faith: A Novel* by Ketty Arucy (2007)
*Who Will Wipe Their Tears? Woman, Girl-Child, Religion, and HIV/AIDS in Africa*
  edited by Esther Mombo and Philemena Mwaura (2007)

# Captive of Fate

**Ketty Arucy, BA**

*Zapf Chancery*
**Eldoret, Kenya**

First Published 2007
© Ketty Arucy
*All rights reserved.*

*Cover Design*
C. B. Peter

*Assdociate Designer*
Michael Nchimbi

*Publishing Consultant*
C. B. Peter

*Printed by*
Kijabe Printing Press,
P. O. Box 40,
Kijabe.

*Published by*

Zapf Chancery Research Consultants and Publishers,
P. O. Box 4988,
Eldoret, Kenya.
Email: zapfchancerykenya@yahoo.co.uk
Mobile: 0721-222 311

ISBN 9966-7185-4-0

# INTRODUCTION

Whenever she thought about her real world, she did it with a certain amount of apprehension. She was very conscious of her own crudity and limitations. Her knowledge and experience may have been restricted by her background, but her vision, never. She had groped almost blindly for education. While other girls of her age craved for satisfaction in cheap, short-term interests, she struggled hard with an inborn obstinacy. With this inborn insight, she chose to take a different path. This combined with her Christian convictions helped her to develop harmonious thoughts in the midst of tribulations. What seemed to be well-regulated feelings had become the inmates of her mind as she continued to attain maturity. She appeared contented, portraying herself as a well disciplined and subdued character.

Life experiences had taught her that the real world was wide and that a varied field of hopes, aspirations, fears and excitements awaited those who had the courage to go forth into its expanse to seek real knowledge of life amidst its perils. Perhaps it was the knowledge of her helplessness in life that had set this type of thinking. Her vision was to rise like Phoenix from the ashes of her present life to the polite respect of the outside world; a world that was as far from her as the jungle of Africa from the developed cities of Europe and America. After experiencing defeat at every turn, she developed her own philosophy about life. Her objective was not to defy it, but to face it with glum stoicism. She would do anything to safeguard this noble secret to the path of success.

# CHAPTER ONE

After a hard day of scrapping the yard and polishing the house in preparation for the Christmas festivities, Ann retired to the bedroom, which she shared with her cousins to rest, and relax her tired muscles. As she drew back the curtain to allow in more light, she noticed a book on the windowsill probably left behind by Clare, her eldest cousin. Tempted by curiosity, she picked the book to read its title but before she could open it, Clare burst in obviously expecting to find her cousin in some mischief that would provide an opportunity for ridicule. She stopped midway through the door when she saw Ann with her book. "What the hell are you doing in the room at this hour?"

Accustomed to molestation and abuse, Ann did not bother to reply. Her only care was how she would endure the insults that would automatically follow the question. Infuriated by the calm on Ann's face, Clare went on; "I am talking to you. Didn't you know that you were relieving the house girl this evening? Answer me!" "I was reading..." Ann tried to explain but ran short of words."

Reading what? Who told you to read that book? It is my book, mark you." She snatched the book from Ann and threw it on her bed. "You ungrateful rat, you have no right to be here in the first place. You should note for one, that you are a dependant. You own nothing and should not touch anything without permission. You are such stress in this house. Don't you have relatives elsewhere to bother other than Mum! Free food, free clothes, free school fees and many other privileges at my mother's expense do not give you the right to do what you want whenever you feel like". Clare paused to look at her cousin's strained face and realising that the ridicule had reached home, she banged the door and left.

Ann tried to remain calm, suppressing her tears as a sign of defiance against her arrogant cousin. It was the only way to hit back, but the question that kept recurring in her mind whenever she went through such moments was, how long was she supposed to endure this?

Two years had elapsed in Mr. Tumbo's house and all that she felt was resentment. Life seemed to get unbearable everyday. She not only felt disappointed but frustrated by the harassment from the entire household. Her daily life consisted of bullying and harassment from everyone in the surrounding. It tormented her even more to realise that instead of protecting her, her Aunt, the only relative who had pretended to care for her by taking her from her parents seemed to delight in wounding her cruelly. If she complained about anything, the response was always the same; " You deceitful brat" or "Your behaviour is unpleasant to everyone here".

As the fifth child from a poor family of seven children, Ann's future seemed uncertain when she began as a child. For her family, education was a luxury. Except for her elder sister Cindy who had succeeded in getting through high school and training as a nurse with support from a paternal Aunt, Ann like her brothers had dropped out of school at the age of twelve to work as a house girl to supplement her mother's limited income.

Remembering with a smile the excitement that had coursed through her body when her Aunt picked her from her home promising to take her to school, Ann wondered why she ever imagined that her problems were over. Considering the harsh and hostile treatment she had to cope with at the moment, her hopes for a brighter future began to diminish. She missed the peace and tranquillity that had prevailed in her childhood despite the impoverished state of her family. In this state, fear gripped in as she began to realise that as much as her present life appeared vague, her future remained uncertain. She felt like a captive in some fate and wished she could predict the outcome."

"Unjust! Unjust!" Ann thought forced by an agonising stimulus power, which instigated some urgent expedient resolution to achieve escape from the insurmountable oppression by either running away or never eating or drinking anymore so that she could die. At this point, tears choked her eyes as she tried to absorb the truth concerning her state. She felt like protesting against such injustice but to whom? She was very conscious of the fact that a moment's mutiny would render her liable to severe penalties. She grieved and regretted the separation from her family but felt helpless as she contemplated the consequences of rebelling and returning home. It would diminish her chances of going to high school, which she was anxiously looking forward to. At this point, she remembered her mother's advice that it was her duty to bear with all situations and never to shy away from problems."

"It is weak and silly to say you can't bear to face your fate." Her mother had told them one evening cautioning them that the future depended entirely on their power of endurance. While this doctrine appeared too complex to comprehend, she could not rule out the underlying truth especially for someone who felt like a captive in some indefinite fate as herself. She could not blot out the fact that her destiny would be shaped by her power to endure. Saddened by the sequence of events in her life, she had to comfort herself by trusting in God. Somehow she believed that through the power of God as preached in the Sunday summons, she would break these chains of undefined bondage and live happily like her tormentors. This thought gave her the strength to endure.

# CHAPTER TWO

November, December and half of January was passing away. Christmas and the new year had been celebrated with the usual festive cheers. Presents had been exchanged while dinner and evening parties were thrown. But for every bit of this enjoyment, Ann had observed from far. Her share of gaiety consisted of witnessing the daily apparelling of her cousins descend to the living room in their tight jeans and colourful T-shirts with matching makeup not forgetting their gallant shoes and elaborately styled hair. Later, she would listen to the sound of the radio or video down stairs amidst the jingling of glasses and Chinaware as refreshments were served to the broken hum of conversation occasionally punctuated by bits of laughter.

Ann felt sad, but not miserable. In reality, she had no wish to be in such company where she would hardly be noticed. The parties involved ladies and gentlemen, not appendages like herself.

On this particular evening, she remained quiet throughout dinner. Her mind dwelt on the fate that underlay her high school education. She had topped her school in KCPE examinations and managed to secure a place in a national school. But this did not seem to change the state of affairs in Mr. Tumbo's house. The cold treatment she received after announcing her results was the least expected. She felt she at least deserved a commendation if not a pat on the back for the outstanding performance. Instead, she could sense resentment. This baffled and upset her. There could only be one reason for this type of reaction on their part. Jealousy.

Two weeks had elapsed since she received an invitation letter to join a national high school in the city for her secondary education. "That school is too expensive. You have to join a cheaper one to avoid unnecessary expenses on my part," her aunt had remarked carelessly on receiving the news. Ann felt hurt but could not dare to show her emotions. Swallowing her bitterness, she wished her aunt had reserved the comment. "It is only three days to the opening date", Ann thought bitterly considering the reluctance portrayed by her aunt over her high school fate. She dreaded to imagine that there was no high school for her after all. Haunted by the fear of ending her education at standard eight, she felt weak, ate less and hardly spoke to anybody. Her curiosity was getting into a state of despair. What would she do if it came to the worst? Why did she have to go through such experiences? Did God exist anyway or it was mere concept in the fertile imagination of some religious scholar trying to find solace in a higher being? She needed clear answers to these questions to spare her the desperation. But none could be found. Excusing herself, she left for the kitchen to finish up her routine chores. She cleared her kitchen chores faster than antici-pated. Looking at the kitchen clock, it was 8p.m. "Too early for bed." She said surveying the weather outside through the window. For a short while, she contemplated joining her hosts in the living room to watch a movie but dismissed the thought quickly. She walked to the back yard through the kitchen door and leaned on the ironing board erected against the kitchen wall.

The weather was friendly with a clear sky full of bright stars and a cold soothing breeze. In her state of mind, this was just what she needed. She stood gazing at the beautiful sky for a while be-fore her tranquillity was interrupted. It was her aunt's sharp voice that brought her back to reality.

"What are you thinking about?" The unexpected company and question took her by surprise.

"Nothing." She said quickly hoping that the response would put her aunt off so that she would leave her alone.

"Nothing! What sort of an answer is that Ann? When I came here you were looking at the sky absent- minded thinking about God knows what. Of late you look disturbed and indifferent. What is up?"

"Nothing auntie. I am sorry if my behaviour has upset you. I only came here to relax." "Well if it's nothing important to talk about,

I have something to tell you". Her aunt said reluctantly. "It is about your high school education. I have found you a good boarding school in Kakamega. I want you to prepare for shopping tomorrow."

Ann shrunk at the revelation perplexed at the unexpected gesture. The surprised look on her face annoyed her aunt who had hoped she would be excited by the news.

"What is wrong with you Ann? Nothing in this world seems to impress you. What kind of human being are you?" Her aunt snapped irritated by her cold response.

"I am sorry auntie". Ann said apologetically running to embrace her aunt in appreciation.

"I just didn't know what to say in response to such wonderful news."

# CHAPTER THREE

It was a hot afternoon despite the cloudy sky. Ann assisted her aunt to offload the luggage from the country bus they had used from the city to her new school. Across the road, she saw a wide black gate with a logo "Knowledge Is Power; Welcome to Matungu Girls High School". Her heart raced with excitement as they stood outside the gate waiting for the security guard to open up for them. She was one week late but it didn't bother her at all. What mattered then was the fact that she was joining high school. She had one goal to pursue and she would do her level best to achieve it in that local school.

When the gate opened, she was amazed to see the beautiful flower gardens in front of the school's administration block. The yard was crowded with students and their parents. They had reported late like her, Ann thought.

"This way Ann", her aunt led her through the crowd toward the offices where some parents were queuing with their daughters. She followed obediently. It was the best day of her life and she was determined to make the best out of it. She knew that it would only take a short while to go through the admission procedures after which, her aunt would leave. And then, it would be herself, her new friends and a new environment; away from the tormenting hostile environment at her aunt's.

"Wake up Ann! It is bath time". The sharp voice woke her up from deep sleep. After an exhausting admission day at the high school, Ann had slept immediately she retired to bed. Thanks a lot to the Headmistress who had appointed mothers from senior classes for Form One students. This made her orientation at the new environment easier. The call was from Pamela, her appointed mother.

Ann woke up and made her bed under Pamela's guidance before they carried their water to the bathrooms. Pamela was motherly and affectionate. Being the Christian Union leader in the school, it was easier for Ann who was a committed Christian to relate with her easily.

After cleaning their cubical at the dormitory, they went for breakfast together and parted for classes after breakfast. Before their departure, Pamela invited Ann to their Christian Union prayers in the evening and she accepted. The prayers normally took place during games time.

When the bell rung at 3.00 p. m, while most of her classmates ran to the sports grounds, Ann went to Pamela's class from where they went together to the meeting hall.

"How long do prayers take?" She asked out of curiosity as they approached Taifa Hall where the prayers were being conducted.

"About an hour. It depends on how the Holy Spirit moves". Pamela replied.

"One hour!" Ann exclaimed remembering how she had struggled in the past to pray for just half an hour.

"It is a bit different from the normal prayers". Pamela explained.

"How different?" Ann asked as she prepared herself for the surprise.

When they entered the hall, some girls were already kneeling on the floor. They all were quiet but with heads and eyes lifted up. Pamela slipped to her knees and did the same.

Ann walked past her friend to the empty space at the corner and knelt down. She waited for a while expecting someone to start praying but nothing happened. As the silence dragged on, she opened her eyes. Everyone's face was lifted up in worship. For a while, she tried to convince herself that this was some type of cult practice and wanted to walk out but something held her down.

She heard a quiet sob and looked up in surprise. It was Pamela crying. As far as she knew, Pamela was not upset about anything. Could she walk over and comfort her? She thought as she looked around to see if the crying touched anyone. Then to her surprise, everyone started to cry, gently at first, but as she watched in curiosity, the crying turned into heavy sobbing and then deep moaning and groaning as though they were desperately upset about something.

So far no words had been spoken.

Suddenly, Pamela fell prostrate on the floor as though in pain. Ann was startled and frightened. Without waiting for more happenings that appeared all strange to her, she gathered all courage and sneaked out quietly, her head reeling with countless questions.

Ann's life in high school was smooth and interesting. Considering her disciplined and mature behaviour, she rose from the ranks of class prefect in Form One, dinning prefect in Form Two and head prefect in Form Three; a rank she retained until the fourth form.

Knowing the limitations of her background and determined to curve a better future, she worked extra hard to balance her academic and leadership demands. At the final end her efforts paid dearly because when her K. C. S. E results came out, she had scored above her expectations.

# CHAPTER FOUR

At the age of 19, Ann looked extremely attractive. She knew it and everybody else did. She was slender and of reasonable height, not too tall and not short to look tiny. She wore long shiny black hair, which fell in cascades at the back of her head and a deep fring down to her eyes brows, which accented her enormous eyes. Her face was perfect with small straight nose and full luscious lips. She never wore makeup but still looked so attractive that people often wondered what a temptress she would be if she wore some. She had just completed her fourth form and was looking forward to joining University.

With pressure from domestic chores following the dismissal of the house girl upon her arrival after her fourth form examinations, Ann hardly had time to ponder over her own problems. Clare appeared wicked than ever. She would cook up all sorts of mischief to have Ann ridiculed or even punished: Her resentment for Ann was so obvious that it was almost palpable. Dismissing her as a dull celibate who had no idea of what her beauty was worth, she wondered how one could be so ignorant of her beauty not to use it to the best advantage. If she had such beauty, Clare thought with admiration, she would bring all men to their knees and get anything she wanted.

On the contrary, Ann resented her cousin's lifestyle regarding her as a spoiled brat who sought for nothing but vainglory. She wondered why rich men's children often took life for granted. From her observation, Clare's lifestyle was one big fun fare of continuous excitement or else, the world would be a dungeon. She had to be admired, courted, flirted with and above all, there had to be music, dancing and society or she would languish in misery and die. The most surprising thing was that her parents did not just approve of it but promoted this behaviour in her cousins through the countless parties thrown at their house.

"This world!" she exclaimed loudly as she went on to straighten the beds in their bedroom.

"What has the world done little Saint?" Clare asked from the doorway after watching her for a while without her knowledge. Without waiting for Ann's response she went on, "I have good news for you tonight Ann. Please don't disappoint me". Ann moved back and sat on her bed wondering what her cousin was up to.

"What about tonight." She asked ignoring Clare's penetrating eyes. "Promise you will say yes first!" Clare insisted. "Okay, I promise to say yes." Ann replied. "That is great then." Clare said cheerfully moving closer to ensure that her mother in the adjacent room did not hear them. "You see," she whispered. "There's this rich guy I met. He's got a posh car and a lot of money. In fact he owns a petrol station at Kayole estate and...."

"Go right to the point Clare." Ann interrupted.Clare would not find the right words to express herself but ignoring Ann's impatient tone, she went on, "Okay, he saw you in one of those photographs we took at Joy's wedding and ...." she hesitated.

"Go on I am listening." Ann said impatiently."You know what? He's fallen for you. He says you're the most gorgeous girl he ever laid eyes on. I promised to organise for you to meet him tonight at the Big Bite. I think this is a golden opportunity for a person like you Ann." Clare concluded hopefully."

What! Save your breath lady. Who do you take me for? Some cheap slut, huh!" Ann fumed.

Ignoring her sentiments Clare went on, "Look here Ann, I..." She was determined to win her cousin over this but now realized it may have been a mistake. Cutting her short, Ann had to make herself clear. She could not endure to listen to this insult any more. Or was it a joke? She thought. "Clare please! I told you to save your breath. My answer is "no" and you can pass my apologies to your friend. If you will excuse me please, I have some work to do." She stood to leave but was roughly pulled back by Clare who was now furious.

"Ann! you had no right to be born, for you make no use of your life." She hissed and shook her violently. Ann tried to pull away to escape from the verbal assault that would follow but Clare's grip on her arm was so hard that it hurt, "Instead of living for yourself as any reasonable being ought to, you seek only to foster your feebleness on my mother's strength." Clare barked. "When she feels unwilling to burden herself with you, you complain and claim you are miserable, neglected and ignored. It is high time you realized your misery is self- inflicted and stop blaming other people. You good for nothing pig!" She let her grip off Ann and walked out.

Ann knew that what Clare had said was true. Her presence in their house had always been treated with disdain and anyone watching would tell that she was more of a liability than an asset. She wished she could escape from this hostile and unwelcoming environment but she couldn't. She had come too far to look back. She thought as she remembered her mother's request for perseverance.

"The fruits of patience lie far much in the future." Her mother had said one day when Ann indicated to her the wish to escape from her aunt's mistreatment.

Whenever she pondered over these words, her desire to give up and rebel vanished. She had always acknowledged the fact that money would bring happiness. She would have loved to have some herself, but for her it had to be earned through honest means. Pretending to fall in love with a man for his wealth was wrong. She knew that such happiness was always short-lived and sometimes ended up in pain or tragically. She was afraid of repercussions like unwanted pregnancy, HIV/Aids and tragic abortions, which result from such relationships. She had to guard herself with all options. To achieve this, she had to stick to her programme which kept her occupied throughout. In this case, she had devised a system which made her independent of all effort and wills but her own. A day for her would be divided into sections, each with a portion of its tasks without leaving any unemployed quarters of any hour. For every quarter, she could perform a task in its turn with methodical and rigid regularity and this way, a day would end without being aware. She could be indebted to no-one for helping her get rid of one vacant moment, sought nobody's company, conversation, sympathy or forbearance.

While devising this system, she had reached the conviction that what drives most people into immoral activities was boredom. If one was idle, she had thought, and went about screwing, whining and socialising like her cousins, then they would suffer the consequences of their actions, however bad and insufferable they appeared. Observing her hosts' lifestyle, she saw them as trapped in a sequence of attention-seeking activities that would end as tragically as a moth to a flame. She wished she could help them perceive life from her point of view but the plain truth was that they would scorn her. Their worlds were not only different but also completely parallel.

# CHAPTER FIVE

The car hooted three times before Ann dropped the pan she was scrubbing and rushed to see who was hooting. She had initially ignored the hooting assuming that it was at the neighbour's gate but the persistency in hooting alerted her and quickened her to go and confirm that it was at their gate.

As she approached the gate, Tumbo emerged from his white saloon car with a big smile on his face. Ann was surprised because normally, it would have been a scowl followed by a ridicule or rebuke.

"Hey sweetheart, what are you doing? I have hooted so many times. I hope I didn't disturb you busy termite." He said jokingly leaning as he leaned against his car. Ann's heart leapt and stopped as she contemplated the implication of the expression sweetheart. She stood there for a while amazed and embarrassed not knowing how to respond.

"Sweetheart!" The words echoed in her mind. Was he serious or just being sarcastic? How could he have changed overnight from the cold, insensitive harasser to a warm loving host? This sudden change surprised Ann because the delight he expressed on seeing her implied something deeper than mere teasing. "But why so sudden?" She asked herself.

For the past six years she had lived in his house, he hardly appeared to notice her existence. Normally, he had treated her more like an object than a human being. If he talked to her, it was either to reprimand, rebuke, insult or give orders. His unexpectedly warm, rarely won smile therefore warned her of possible trouble, which lay ahead. She had to be careful. Ann thought as she proceeded to open the gate.

As she went on with her chores in the kitchen, Ann felt disturbed by the obvious expression of lust in Tumbo's behaviour. The truth behind this thought scared her. How was she going to cope? She asked herself. Lust like smoke could hardly be confined. Sooner or later, her aunt would notice and then, God knows what would follow. She had to do something about this situation before it got out of control. But what could she do? After serious thinking she realized that nothing much could be done to stop his pursuit if her imagination was right. Whatever the case, she resolved to improvise a way of handling the situations as they came. Her only hope was to trust God to cover the situation so that her aunt, would not notice what was happening. Meanwhile, she would keep ignoring him until he gave up. In the blankness of this shock, only a veneer of basic manners would carry her through such trying moments.

Two weeks passed without a similar recurrence and Ann began to convince herself that she could handle the situation without raising eyebrows. She had reorganised her routine duties to avoid him as much as possible and somehow the scheme had worked. What she did not realise however was the nature of patience sugar daddies sustain when they develop interest in young women. As it turned out later, Tumbo was only buying time to allow her calm down and get used to the new scenerio. Like a hunter, he had laid his trap and was waiting for the opportunity to spring up and grab his prey.

Christmas was approaching. Ann had to work extra hard to keep up with her domestic chores' demands. Occasionally, she worked late past midnight.

On the other hand, Tumbo's sexual drive towards her was pressing past his possible control. He had to do something to escape loss of his sanity. One evening while he sat watching a movie a thought came to his mind. He had noticed Ann work late past midnight when everyone had retired to bed. His wife left for bed earlier on most occasions possibly out of exhaustion and wouldn't be much of a problem in this case. His problem therefore would be the children but they were always out socialising. This left him with the possibility that once his wife went to bed; he could make a move to sort out his problem with Ann. But how successful would this move be and what would be the consequences if it failed? He asked himself pretending to concentrate on the movie on the screen.

Where love is involved, reason has no business. The drive within him towards Ann was too strong to resist. There was only one way out? To take the risk and endure whatever consequences that awaited him ahead.

As she emerged from the bathroom with a towel round her waist, Ann heard footsteps on the stairs coming from the sitting room. The bathroom was situated between their bedroom and her Aunt's. In this case, their doors were adjacent. With dim light penetrating through the upper glass on their bedroom door to light the corridor, she could easily identify the person. Pulling up the towel from her waist to cover her bare bosom, she stood still in the half open bathroom door waiting for whoever was on the stairs to emerge. She had expected everyone except herself to be asleep.

The sight of Tumbo in transparent nylon pyjamas sent shock waves through her body. She nearly screamed when she saw the triumphant smile on his face but she couldn't. A chilly feeling went down her spine as she attempted to retreat into the bathroom and shut the door. Sensing her intentions, he moved swiftly and pushed the door before she was able to lock it. The door slammed back and pushed Ann to hit the back wall and while she attempted to steady herself, he grabbed her violently, hugging her naked body passionately, so hard that she felt pain all over. She struggled to pull away in vain and before she could even think of screaming, her mouth was covered with his as he tried to kiss her forcibly. Panting like a dog that had been chasing a prey for a long distance, he pushed her violently to the wall. " He must be insane." Ann thought as she desperately contemplated on the possible move to escape from this insanity. She felt weak and dizzy but her desire to fight on persisted. When her struggle turned into despair, she felt her knees give way followed by a blanket of darkness.

Tumbo felt her body relax and her head's collapse on his shoulder. His excitement increased thinking that she had finally given in but was surprised when he felt her lifeless hands drop by her sides.

"Oh God, don't let her die." He gasped in panic on realisation that she was unconscious. Lifting her carefully, he placed her on the wet floor to check her pulse. His desire had vanished and his mind cleared. He groped in the darkness for the electrical switch on the wall so as to get enough light. It took him longer than necessary to trace it following the panic that had engulfed him. As he reached for the switch, he suddenly changed his mind. It would be safer to handle her in the darkness, he resolved. Bending over her bare body, he once more clumsily checked for the heartbeat and the pulse in her veins near the wrist.

"Oh! She's fine." His heart leaped with excitement when he felt the steady pulse. What should he do? He asked himself. He had to think fast to get himself out of the mess. With the lusty urge quenched, the feel of her body made him feel disgusted. He lifted her prostrate body slightly to wrap the towel around her waist. When he had finished, he laid her on her back with the feet facing the door to make it look like she had a sliding fall on the slippery floor. Convinced of the reality of his scheme, he leapt out of the bathroom confidently shutting the door behind him and sneaked into his bedroom.

Half an hour elapsed before Ann regained full consciousness. Chilled by the wet floor, she shivered uncontrollably. "What happened?" She asked herself struggling to recall what had transpired. Then, she began to remember every scene as they rehearsed in her mind. Struggling to her feet, she steadied herself on the nearby sink to avoid falling. Her desire was to switch on the light and check her appearance in the mirror. The sight of her frightened eyes made her feel sick. Gathering the only strength left in her body, she switched off the light and fled from the bathroom leaving the door wide open.

Hot tears burnt her eyes as she entered the bedroom. Her knees were weak and trembling. She had to force herself to stand steadily and dress up for bed. Throwing the towel across the room, she picked her nightdress from the nearby hanger and broke into sobs as she put it on.

"What is up Ann?" Lyn asked, awakened by her sobs. "Another moment of insanity, isn't it? What causes the stress?" She asked hoping it would stop Ann from sobbing. But she was wrong. Ann's sobs turned hysterical leaving Lyn disgusted. Expecting any response at the moment was hopeless. Lyn thought as she jumped out of bed to switch off the light.

Ann could not find sleep. She kept wondering what lay ahead in Tumbo's house after that night's experience. She had miraculously missed a rape ordeal but there was no confirmation that it wouldn't happen again. She had to come up with a solution to her new crisis but didn't seem to think of any. Would it be right to narrate the ordeal to her aunt? She asked herself. "No!" the reply was almost instant in her mind. Her aunt would never believe her. The possible reaction could be worse than the ordeal itself, she reminded herself.

Hoping that no one else had witnessed the traumatic experience, she resolved to shut her mouth on the issue and pretend that it never happened.

*Captive of Fate*

# CHAPTER SIX

Always busy; no time for rest. Too much work makes Ann a dull girl." Tumbo remarked standing behind Ann. A week had passed since that dreadful night when his attempts to have a little fun with her almost ended up tragically. At first he had been too embarrassed to approach her. Whenever he thought of that experience, he felt disgusted, but to his surprise, Ann looked calm and composed. Nobody could tell that anything horrible had happened between them. Tumbo wondered how she could be so strong to brush aside such an encounter without causing any trouble.

As time went by, he began to admire her again. What disturbed him more was the urge to hold her again. How would he go about it this time? Would she let him get away with it again as she had done before? This obsession was driving him crazy. For the last two days, he seemed to have lost focus in his normal operations. His level of concentration had dropped to minimal. After spending a few sleepless nights and trying to concentrate a whole morning in vain, he resolved to excuse himself from the office and drive home to sort himself out.

Tumbo let himself in quietly when he found the gate unlocked. He packed his car and resolved to enter the house through the backdoor. He found Ann washing clothes in the backyard. "How are you dearest?" He said jokingly to provoke her into a conversation. Ann jumped surprised by the unexpected arrival of her host. She had never seen him come home before five o'clock on working days. Wiping her soapy hands on the apron, she moved a few steps away remembering what had happened a few days back.

"Oh! Good afternoon Mr. Tumbo". She greeted him ignoring his remark. "You are early today. Why didn't you hoot...?" Ann stopped short of words. She didn't know what to say in real sense.

"Don't worry". Tumbo interrupted. " I found the gate unlocked and decided to save you the trouble. Tomorrow being Christmas day, I know how busy you are. However, I wouldn't mind a cup of tea. I am very thirsty!" He said this when he noticed her uneasiness. "And by the way, don't forget to lock up the gate." He strode into the house and left Ann standing still.

Ann looked at the dirty utensils in the sink and felt embarrassed, as Mr. Tumbo had used the kitchen entrance to the house. He might wonder what she had been doing the whole morning she thought. As she waited for the water to boil, she decided to clear the sink of the dirty utensils.

In the bedroom, Tumbo placed his suitcase on his wife's dressing table and proceeded to take off his tie and coat. Feeling relieved, he sat on the bed contemplating on what he could do. First, he had to enquire about his children's whereabouts to ensure that they were not at home. "Where is Lyn and Clare?" He asked loudly as he descended the stairs. "I don't know. They left at around 10 am this morning." Ann shouted back.

The water was boiling. She moved swiftly to switch off the kettle and returned to the sink. As she bent to pick a clean cup from the cupboard below the sink, Tumbo grabbed her from behind. Startled by his action, she stood abruptly and tried to push him backward so that she could find room to escape but it was too late. "Shall I scream?" Ann thought frantically but ruled out the thought immediately. It was pointless because no one would bother to rush to her rescue in their kind of neighbourhood where everyone stayed enclosed in locked up compounds. There was only one way out. She had to fight for her safety.

Ann tried every move possible to get out of Tumbo's grip but in vain: Experienced as he was, he was determined to use every tactic to get her. Taking advantage of his superior strength, he turned her round to face him and slapped her face. As she wretched in pain, he cupped her left breast with his right hand and tightened his left hand round her waist. Pain and excitement intermingled, playing havoc on her sensory system. In this confusion, she groaned and took her hands off his chest. Her eyes were tightly shut. Convinced of her surrender, Tumbo pushed her near the kitchen table and began to make loose of his trousers belt.

"Look! It is not big Ann. It won't hurt you. If only you could relax." Tumbo cooed persuasively.Ann opened her eyes to see what he meant. Embarrassed by the shameless act, she shut her eyes again and felt dizzy. She wanted to faint but some voice inside urged her to steady herself and fight on. "Don't give in. This man will defile you and kick you out. Resist, if possible to the point of death." It urged her on.

When he bent to lift her skirt, Ann saw a frying pan nearby. Her hands were free and driven by instinct, she picked it quickly and hit his head. Shocked by this move, his excitement transformed into fury and disgust. He would have strangled her to death if he got the opportunity but there wasn't. Grabbing her shoulders and shaking her violently he slapped her again but before he could repeat the slap Ann gathered all the saliva in her mouth and spit on his face. Blinded by the saliva, Tumbo felt disgusted and staggered backwards wiping his face with the back of his left hand. "You shameless bitch!" He muttered as he wiped his face with his loosened shirt. "I will strangle you today."

Ann moved away from him but did not think of running off. She should have but she couldn't. It was as though some force was holding her back to fight on. She was trembling out of shock and to steady herself, she moved to the nearby wall and leaned on it for support. Unconsciously, she stood there and watched him wash his face on the sink until he was convinced it was free of her disgusting saliva. When he finished, he picked the kitchen towel on the hook near her to wipe himself. Ann moved towards the table again and stood next to the cooker. As she stood there, a thought of a second attack alerted her to take off but it was too late. Tumbo stood between her and the door fuming. She had to do something if he attacked again. Looking around, she saw a wine bottle on the shelf above the cooker and wondered how she could make use of it.

In one swift move Tumbo slapped her violently. Blinded by the slap and in pain Ann staggered and grabbed the cooker for support. Pleased with the effect of the slap, he moved back and watched her cringe. Pain penetrated her brain paralysing every part of her body. At this moment she realized how helpless it was to fight a strong man and thought of succumbing but something urged her to resist on to the last bit of her consciousness. She opened her eyes hoping that he was gone but to her surprise, he was there smiling triumphantly. "Heartless beast." Ann thought bitterly. Why couldn't he leave her alone?

Reassessing her recovery from the pain, Tumbo moved to hit her again but in a swift move driven by desperation she bent backward avoiding the slap by inches. Tumbo moved back surprised by her brightness and before he could hit her again, she picked the wine bottle from the open shelf and smashed it over his head. Blood oozed like fresh water from a water spring. Tumbo staggered back and escaped through the sitting room door. Ann felt startled by her action. She must have been mad she thought. What if she had killed him? She asked herself stricken by panic. How was she going to sort out this mess? A sixth sense warned her that he might retaliate when the pain subsided. She had to run for her life. Ann fled through the gate and crossed the road dangerously without checking for on coming vehicles. She ran towards the main gate. Her blood- stained blouse was wide open but she didn't care. She would have been knocked down by Mrs. Tumbo's approaching car if she hadn't broken off abruptly to avoid hitting her. Noticing that the victim was her niece, Jane panicked as she drove into her parking yard. What could have happened? She wondered. Were there thugs in her house? Accepting the possibility she reversed abruptly and parked her car outside the neighbour's gate. For a while, she sat confused, not knowing what to do. Finally, she stepped out of her car and walked towards the crowd gathering at the estate entrance. Ann's shocking appearance had attracted a mild crowd. She was stopped by the security guards who wanted to know what had transpired at the house. Briefed by the guards on what was reported to have happened, her aunt felt angry. How could her husband do something like that? Was there a possibility that her niece had intentionally exaggerated the incident for some unknown reason? She asked herself trying to steady her confused mind. "Thanks for your assistance." She told the guards indicating that she wanted to take up the matter herself. "I will sort it out."

She pulled her scared niece from the crowd and dragged her towards the house. Ann resisted all the way. A new thing for her and a circumstance that greatly strengthened the bad opinion her aunt would have disposed to entertain of her. She was strife beside herself though very conscious of the fact that a moment's mutiny had already rendered her liable to severe penalties. But like any other rebel, she felt resolved in her desperation to go all the length and fight, even if it meant losing her privileges for good.

As Ann had predicted, the verdict favoured her offender. After long heart breaking interrogation, the blame ended up on her side. She was to suffer severe penalties, which included two days of confinement in the servant's quarters without food or drink.

As she lay in bed weak and emaciated, sad memories intermingled and cris-crossed her mind. The tyranny in Tumbo's house, her noble relatives proud indifference, evasion and partiality churned up in her disturbed mind like dark deposits in a turbid well. Why was she always the victim? Why was she always suffering being brow beaten, accused and condemned forever? Why could she never please or win favour?

Ann tried to find answers to these questions in vain. Not even to one of them. Her head still ached from the blows and falls she received during her rebellion. No one had reproved Tumbo for the crime. Not even his wife whose trust he had betrayed. She had transgressed against the master and had to suffer the consequences.

"Unjust! Unjust", she thought forced by an agonising stimulus, which instigated some strange expediency to achieve escape from insupportable oppression. Her brain was in tumult and her heart in insurrection. She wished she could answer the ceaseless inward questions: "Why?" and "For how long?"

*Captive of Fate*

# CHAPTER SEVEN

As she sat amidst a handful of students in the university library, Ann thought sadly of the child she had been and the lessons she had learned as she grew up. Her admission to the university had been a dream fulfilled but the lessons she had gone through had not been good ones. They had not been the ordinary learning experiences of most children, she thought. Life had taught her that the world was a jungle and that love had no meaning, no place and no function. For her love could neither feed her, support her, nor protect her from the harsh realities of life.

She tried to concentrate on the page she had just opened and tried to understand what the author was discussing on the topic, "Man and Religion" but could grasp nothing. Dissatisfied with the author's arguments, she closed the book and picked another one, "Man and his origin." She opened the book and tried to study some archaeological findings elaborated by pictures from various scholars but her mind kept on straying back to the past. Eventually, she drifted back completely burying her mind in the past memories.

Looking deep within herself made her feel dizzy and unhappy. It was preferable, she thought with a wry irony, to skate along the surface of life and ignore the cracking ice beneath. She looked back at herself as a child and saw a little girl carefully picking her way through debris of a terrain that was rough, barren and ugly. Was it any wonder that she had learnt to be aloof and suspicious? And should it come as a surprise that she had no friends! Inside she felt empty and alone; angry at the fact that despite all the barricades she had erected around herself, she still felt insecure. She had begun to realise and believe that life was nothing but a series of chaotic events that could not bring happiness to anyone. If you were born in the right family, then you were fortunate and could be successful and contented. But if you grew up as she had in a poor family, your life was bound to be rough and difficult. You had to struggle for survival. Accepting this reality, she could take nothing for granted, not good luck, happiness, or even success. Such things were short-lived, she thought and this inspired her to work even harder. Inside, she knew that she could trust no one to help her achieve what she wanted. The burden of success had always fallen completely on her shoulder. She avoided cultivating any acquaintances because life had developed in her a hands-off attitude, self-reliance and self-consciousness. Was it any wonder that she was fiercely independent! She thought. She feared dependency and would do everything possible to keep her admirers at bay, especially men. "Men aren't worth trusting." She remembered her mother's comment one evening and smiled at the thought.

Suddenly, the library bell rung alerting students that it was time to leave. Pushing back her chair, she picked up her folder and left for the hostel. "Thank God the day is over." Ann sighed loudly throwing her pocket file on the bed as she contemplated on the next move. She had returned from her last class feeling exhausted from the trips made in the course of her lessons as she moved from one lecture theatre to another. She had one hour left before dinner and wondered what she would do to occupy herself.Spending it in the room was out of question considering the surrounding.

Three beds away from hers lay Mutinda in bed scratching her boyfriend's bare feet. On the opposite end was Achieng absorbed in a movie on her 4 by 4 inch television undisturbed by her neighbours.

"This is truly hell on earth." Ann thought, disgusted by Mutinda's shameless behaviour. She resented her roommates' behaviour but could do nothing considering the limited accommodation space in the crowded Campus. Such behaviour was completely unappealing and irresponsible, she convinced herself.        Mutinda    and Achieng were reckless. If they were not drinking alcohol, smoking or playing loud music, they would either be in bed with their lovers or entertaining a team of rowdy friends.Cherono and Wairimu were attached to each other and hardly stayed in the room. Sharing the same combination of subjects, they went for classes together, ate together, worked together, and studied together. Amina spend the least time in the room. On most occasions, she would only come in to change her clothes, pick a few others and disappear without a greeting to her roommates. This left Ann without company.

She would have preferred to spend the remaining one-hour resting in bed but the environment was uninviting. Achieng increased the volume of her radio cassette system possibly to reduce the distraction from the neighbouring bed but continued with her concentration on the television screen. If Ann wished to stay in that room, she would have to close her eyes and cover her ears so as to have peace. Checking her watch again she realised that it would be cartoon time on the college television in the common room. This meant the room was virtually empty and would be the best place to resort to.

As she lay on the couch in the empty room, she thought about how lonely she was. Though accustomed to solitary life throughout her childhood, Ann began to realise that avoiding friendship in this type of environment was almost impossible. Socialisation was the culture in her new environment. On most occasions, she had to force herself to cope with the embarrassment of seeing her colleagues kiss in public. How can they be so shameless? She had asked herself several times whenever she saw her friends kissing in the lecture theatres.

A team of rowdy male students who invaded the common room interrupted her thoughts. Without hesitation she sat up and waited to see what they were up to. "Turn to Metro bwana. It's Ras time. This lady should be crazy watching cartoon." The comment was an intentional provocation and Ann stood to leave without uttering a word. The last thing she wanted was a confrontation with college boys. When she got to her room, it was locked from inside. She didn't bother knocking because Mutinda would never open. She checked her watch and realised that it was only five minutes left before dinner. She had intended to dash for an early dinner and rush to the library but it would not be possible. Her money for dinner was in the room.

'Shameless slut!' Ann muttered as she walked towards the rear door to wait in the backyard until her room was accessible. Full of anger, she felt miserable. Hot tears burnt her eyes but she wouldn't let them out. Other girls might notice her misery and make a scene, she thought. She had to do something but what? She thought. As she approached the door, her eyes were blind with tears and the only sensible thought that came to her mind was to rush into the laundry room and wash her face. It was right opposite the back door.

# CHAPTER EIGHT

L adies and gentlemen, I am grateful this morning to have the pleasure of opening this important discussion. First of all, I wish to thank doctor Ayot for giving me the opportunity to introduce the subject on her behalf. The topic is, " Women and rape: Who should be blamed? I am not only persuaded but convinced that women are to blame for the escalating cases of sexual violence in our society." There was applause and protest from the audience but he ignored and continued.

"Sexual harassment may occur when a person is sexually provoked. The provocation may take different forms. Young men, what would you do for instance if a half-naked woman wearing a mini-skirt and a mini-blouse or a tight skirt with a sky-high slit or a skin tight, peddle pusher, a spaghetti top or a sheer transparent dress passed in front of you or sat next to you?" He paused for a while but did not wait for a reaction.

"Let me tell you ladies what happens. The sight of what I have just described will drive any normal man crazy. He may not just feel confused emotionally but he is psychologically tormented. The strain of a sexual drive is uncontrollable and the only solution is to find a way to let it out. According to my conviction, women should be blamed but on most occasions it is the man who is blamed and punished, even when it happens between a sexually deprived husband and an insensitive wife. Surely the world is headed for doom."

"Explain further. What do you mean?" Dr. Ayot inspired him to continue when she realised that he had exhausted his ideas.

"What I mean is that the issue of 'rape' in marriage as alleged by feminists is unfounded and insane. How can you forcibly take what is lawfully yours? In marriage the woman legally belongs to the man and sexual intercourse is a husband's right not a privilege."

"Oh! I disagree with that but I will reserve my comments for now. Class do you agree with him?" Dr. Ayot asked the students, who reacted differently.

The speaker was Dr. Kombo. He had been invited by Dr. Ayot to discuss an article, which had appeared in one of the local newspapers after establishing that he was the author.

"No I disagree." Ann shouted.

"Okay class, let Ann tell us her view". Dr. Ayot said trying to calm down the noisy audience.

Ann walked slowly but confidently to the front while Kombo went for the seat at the far end where he sat next to Dr. Ayot. Placing her notes on the table, she looked around the room to study the reaction of her classmates. Her eyes rested on Dr. Kombo for a while before proceeding with her argument. Kombo's eyes met hers. She looked more attractive than he had anticipated; he thought silently. From his observation, she wore a Madonna kind of look; a look that portrayed a naïve sensual woman not a radical feminist as Ann was usually referred to around the campus.

"Dear colleagues" Ann started and paused briefly to allow her excited audience to calm down. "I am not just surprised but astonished by what I have just heard. Rape is a social evil, which has seriously affected our society. Its implications aren't just scary but should be seen as intolerable in any civilised society. If I were given time to describe it, I wouldn't hesitate to assert that it is worse than murder because the victim has to live with this horrible experience for the rest of her life. Don't get me wrong." Ann cautioned her audience. "I do not disagree with the fact that indecent dressing can provoke rape but what I cannot overlook is the fact that these rapes mostly occur to innocent old women and children; basically in environments where indecent dressing is hardly a factor like villages. How for instance, can we account for cases where fathers raped their daughters, majors raped minors, young men raped old women or even animals like cows and chickens?" She asked the audience drawing laughter from her colleagues.

"How does this behaviour relate to sexual provocation? Should we assume that men are provoked by animals and birds too?"

Without giving room for response she proceeded to conclude her argument.

"In my perception, if indecent dressing was the sole cause of rape, more rape cases would have been reported in colleges and city streets than in the villages. How many ladies walk-half naked in this compound or to be precise in this class?" She asked rhetorically.

Kombo looked at Ann in disbelief. She had proved smarter than he had expected. How could she be so pretty and yet so radical?

Dismissing his argument as biased and chauvinistic, she went on with her conclusion arguing that the problem had more to do with social disintegration which she regarded as a stage in social development indicating that the Kenyan society had reached the final level of its civilization, and that the disintegration should be regarded as a natural development which paves ways for the development of a new society.

"If nakedness provokes sexual drive as defined by our friend," she said sarcastically, "Then more cases of rape should have been reported in our grandfathers' days because our grandparents walked more naked than we do today. Or should we assume that they were abnormal and insensitive?" Her stunning conclusion left her audience laughing.

As she left for her seat, Kombo felt challenged but not defeated. He was intrigued by her devastating combination of beauty, brains and communication skills. He felt indifferent about her too and wondered. Instead of despising her for humiliating him over his article, he felt drawn to her and wished to learn more about her personality. He resolved to use every means available to get to know her better.

He was forty and looked it but he never let his age interfere with his personal feelings. Ann might have looked young enough to be his daughter but he was in love and nothing would stop him from going after her.

*Captive of Fate*

# CHAPTER NINE

"This is a lovely park." Ann remarked as she stepped out of the car. It was her first visit to Uhuru Park and the general outlook of the park looked attractive and exciting to her eyes.

"This way Ann." Dr. Kombo led her towards a picnic table on the western side of the swimming pool. It was his first date with Ann and he was determined to make it interesting hoping that it would encourage her into accepting more of such adventures in future. As they opened their picnic packages Ann discovered that he had brought an appetizing packed meal of fried chicken and French fries. Besides, there were pints of passion juice, which she loved.

"How do you find my taste Ann?" Kombo asked while filling her plate. "Oh! This is fantastic" she replied. "It is my favourite." After handing the plate to her, he served himself and went around the table to sit on the opposite bench facing Ann directly. For a while, they ate quietly. When she was halfway through her plate of French fries she looked at Kombo and noticed that he was absorbed in thought.

"Excuse me sir! What are you thinking about?" She asked after looking at him for a while. He must have been completely absent-minded because he didn't seem to notice it. Feeling guilty, he pulled her hand into his and looked straight into her face. "Thinking about you sweetheart."

"That is not true." Ann protested. "You are just a crooked old man who fancied me after I challenged your article that day in H8. You had to devise another strategy to console your ego and it is what you are doing now. Feeling great, isn't it?"

"No. That is a black lie. I fell in love with you the first day I set my eyes on you. Please don't make me cry." He teased her.

Ann smiled but said nothing. She actually felt confused. On accepting a date with this man, she had hardly thought of the implications. For her, it was just a friendly outing together. But there he was declaring his open love for her. Was she ready to handle that kind of commitment? And how was she going to handle it without interfering with her other interests? She asked herself silently.

"Please Ann; say something." He said stroking the back of her left palm.

"What do you expect me to say Dr. Kombo?" She asked him not knowing what he exactly meant by his statement.

"Tell me about yourself Ann, your past or anything interesting.

"Ann looked at him surprised by the unexpected question. Why would he wish to hear about her personal life? She remained quiet for a while trying to decide what she could tell him and where to begin.

"I am waiting Ann!" he persisted. Pressed by his persistence, she sensed the seriousness of his joke and decided to respond.

"When I was young, my life wasn't interesting to be real. In fact I never thought I would be where I am today." She stopped not quite sure whether Kombo wanted her to discuss her early life.

"Do you really want to hear more about my lurid background?" She asked him fearing that he would be bored.

"Yes, everything." He assured her. Ann smiled at the encouragement and proceeded to explain her memorable experiences.

Kombo looked at his watch and shook his head. It was half past three. They had spent two hours unknowingly while they discussed their past. He had intended to take her for a movie and they had half an hour to catch up with the movie. "Eat up dear. There is a couple of old movies at Nairobi Cinema this afternoon, which I want you to see. If we hurry up, we can catch the first one. Please finish up your meal." He urged her realising that her plate still had some food.

Ann felt excited at the proposal because she had always yearned for that kind of treat. She couldn't wait any longer. "I think I am full." She said standing to confirm that she was ready to leave.

Hand in hand they walked to the car park where he had parked his brand new Peugeot. Ann handed him the paper bag containing the picnic left overs which he placed on the back seat after opening the door for her to sit on the front left seat. He then closed the door and went round to open his. "A perfect gentleman." Ann thought.

Throughout the picnic meal, Kombo had restrained from showing any intimacy for fear of scaring Ann away. He wanted her to trust him; to build confidence in his company before he would expose his feelings. But as he sat beside her in the car park outside the cinema hall the urge to hold her increased. He couldn't suppress it any more. Just before he got out to open the door for her, he turned round and kissed her passionately.

Ann felt embarrassed and cried, "Stop it." "I can't stop Ann," he murmured and continued.

"Please don't," she pleaded pushing him away. He continued kissing her sensitive skin ignoring her resistance. When he finally stopped, Ann felt confused by the excitement she had felt when he kissed her. Noticing the confusion in her frightened eyes he pulled her to himself and hugged her for a while.

"Don't be afraid Ann. I love you and I will do everything to make you happy." He assured her. At those words, she relaxed. Kombo noticed her surrender and sighed. Pushing her a few inches back he looked into her eyes admiringly. "You are lovely. I will never have enough of you Ann." He said, his eyes hazy with desire.

"I hope not," she whispered back. Without adding a word, he opened his door and walked round to open hers.

Slipping unseen over the maroon velvet cord roping off the stairs to the balcony, they settled in the front seats. The house lights dimmed and a hush fell over the sparsely filled theatre. Ann could feel her excitement build, as the screen came live with the larger than life characters. She leaned back in her red plush seat to let herself be filled with the make believe-drama unfolding before her.

Kombo slid one arm round her shoulders and she relaxed against it. In the isolated darkness of the Balcony with exotic scenes setting flickering on the screen before her, she felt as if she were slipping into a dream world, an illusion where everything was right and wonderful. She shivered with the beauty of it.

"Are you feeling cold?" Kombo rubbed his broad hands up and down her arms to warm her. "No I am fine." "Sure, sure." He pulled her into the circle of his arms, her back against his chest. She fit there so easily and so naturally as if they were two parts of one perfect puzzle.

"You smell good," he said. "Like flowers growing in the garden."

"Shh! We are missing the movie." Ann said cautiously. In reality, Ann could hardly concentrate on the movie. She wanted to listen to the rumble sound of Kombo's voice as he whispered into her hair. She slipped her hand into his, needing more of him. His palm was broad and warm. His fingers played with hers an erotic dance destroying all power of rational thought. Pictures from the scenes staggered across the screen in one large blur. She had trouble following the movie any further.

Kombo's mind struggled for a while to focus on the movie but instead he preferred to centre his attention on the piece of work in his mind. She plagued him and delighted him. He had never felt like this before with another woman; wanting to be near her, the sound of her voice, her touch… Everything about her drove him wild. At the age of forty, he felt like an adolescent.

He tried to absorb himself in the movie, hoping the action on the screen would dowse the fires of passion that she had set. For a while, it worked until the love scene. The passion on the screen only increased his acute awareness of the woman he held in his arms.

"Let us get out of here." He said when he was no longer able to endure. He only waited while she gathered up her purse and they made an escape out into the bright light outside.

# CHAPTER TEN

Loud music booming from the next room woke Ann from deep sleep. Her eyes felt heavy. "What time is it?" She asked loudly without realising that she was alone in the room. Faith and Grace were out for the weekend. She pulled her head from under the sheets and looked at the alarm clock on the table beside her bed. It was 9.00 am. "Oh God!" She exclaimed realising that she was late for the Sunday service. She had been awake half the night nursing her guilty conscience. Remorse and regret had kept her company as well and they were still exacting their penalties this morning. The previous evening's date had been wild and crazy. Her head thumped as if it had a pulse of its own. She knew that the type of relationship she had got into was wrong. From her Christian convictions, it was immoral. "Oh God! Have mercy upon me." Ann prayed gathering strength to sit up in bed. She struggled to put the ill-fated consequences of the previous day's date out of her mind but found the attempt futile. Her failing emotions ached in her mind. She had always kept her dates cool and uncomplicated but this man threatened to turn her life inside out. He actually had power to steal her heart.

Wondering if a couple of aspirins would sedate her, she felt like her mind was a tangle mass of goosed wires. She had no memory of getting undressed for bed or locking the door. She couldn't even recollect when she returned to the room. All she could recall was a fresh memory of the previous evening's events.

What in God's name had got into her? She asked herself. She didn't even know this man well! A groan escaped her mouth when she realised that she hadn't even switched off the light.

As she woke up to switch it off, she pushed her fingers through her hair that now no longer lay in the classic knot she had dressed it the previous day. In fact the clip was missing. Vaguely she recalled Kombo removing it while at the same time kissing her before he said goodnight. "Oh Lord," she groaned again. She didn't want to think about it. But fighting with all the will at her command wouldn't stop those wonderful moments from storming in. Nothing would oust the memories of the way Dan Kombo seemingly without effort had made her like putty in his hands.

Her watch indicated 9.30 a. m. After switching off the light, she went to unlock the door to avoid disturbance from her roommates' knocks on their return but to her amazement she found it open. "Jesus! The door remained unlocked throughout the night. I should have been damn crazy!" She cursed. Back to her bed, she took two piritons with a cup of orange juice and returned to sleep.

It was 4.30 p.m. when she finally woke up. Astonished at the tiredness of her body, she remembered the events of the previous evening again and felt angry. The unbelievability of her own wayward emotions hit her and then she became aware that she had company. Faith was sitting on the edge of her bed reading a Bible.

"Thank God you are awake at last", said beaming Faith. She went and placed her Bible on the table and came back to plant herself on Ann's bed. "Ever since I came in, you have been dead to the world but seemed to be alive elsewhere. I have never seen you sleep with emotion as you did today. What's up Ann? Is it Kombo?" Faith asked with concern on her face. "I…" Ann began, her mind coming to life and thinking that since Faith was aware of their relationship and was anxious, she might as well tell her the truth that she indeed was in love with Kombo. For sometime she had managed to convince her roommates that he was just a friend.

Looking at Ann directly in the face and shaking her head in disbelief, Faith's conviction of Ann's way-wardness was obvious in her eyes. "I thought I saw something unique between you two. But Jesus Christ Ann, I never expected you to get involved that far. Remember your testimony. You are a Christian for God's sake."

Faith said feeling angry at the confusion in Ann's eyes.

Ann closed her eyes feeling faint. She kept her eyes closed as surging anger gave faintness a hiding. She didn't doubt he was a smug. He seemed determined to control her regardless of her efforts to resist. "Oh God, help me," Ann prayed silently.

"Please, don't go to sleep again Ann," Faith wailed. "I am waiting impatiently to know the whole truth. Although Kombo does not look like one to show emotion in public, he looks as though he has a share in your creamery the way I see. I want you to deny it now.

"Ann opened her eyes but no concrete idea formed. Faith looked so concerned that it caused her to feel annoyed; annoyed with Kombo because of the trouble he was causing her. She wished she had never met him.

"There's nothing to tell you Faith," she said trying to make her voice light. Dan Kombo might have thought he was getting her anywhere he wanted, she thought. Well, he was in for a surprise. He would get her nowhere near the Altar. She didn't even wish to visit him any more.

"Tell me dear," Faith persisted. "How do you feel about him?"

"All that I can say is that he is peculiar though I can't say I have known him well." Ann explained.

"In what way is he peculiar?" Faith asked. "I don't know. It is not easy to describe. Nothing striking, but you feel it when he speaks to you."

"By the way, aren't you the one who told me that you didn't believe in falling in love? Say something Ann!" she demanded.

"You can't always be sure whether he is in jest or earnest or whether he is pleased or the contrary. You don't thoroughly understand him. In short, at least I don't. But it is of no consequence; he is a good man."

"How good?" Faith persisted.

"Mm… Kind and generous." Ann replied reluctantly"

Sure. Kindness and generosity are two distinct features of sugar daddies. Just take care and ensure that you are not swayed from your Christian faith. Remember God hates sin: As the Bible says, the devil comes but to steal, to kill and to destroy. I am not trying to interfere, but I don't want to see you get hurt. You know how much I care about you Ann." Faith said standing to leave.

"And by the way," she said after moving a few feet away. People say that he is one of those guys whose hobby is womanising. Rumour has it that he's dating several girls from your class; Jane. Lilian and Rina included. So take care." Faith said as she opened the door to leave.

A few minutes later, she returned with her electric kettle full of water. "Ann, why can't you take a bath while I prepare a cup of coffee for you. It might improve your state." Faith said placing the kettle on the shelf.

Gathering all the strength left in her weak body, Ann stepped out of bed, picked her soap from under her bed and the towel from the wardrobe and left for the bathroom without saying a word.

# CHAPTER ELEVEN

Ann felt she had reached some sort of cross roads in her life. She had to decide whichever road was favourable but could not rule out the possibility of choosing the wrong one. She knew that she loved Kombo too much to admit yet the circumstances seemed to dictate that she drops him. It would be for her own good, she thought. She had at least managed to avoid him for a week but this hadn't favoured her psychologically. Remembering the sleepless nights and the poor concentration in her academic work when her mind strayed to think about Kombo, Ann doubted if she would ever succeed in cutting him out of her life completely. Sometimes the temptation to go and see him made her life unbearable. But she had decided to take her roommate's advice to keep off Kombo seriously.

"Ann, here is your note. Rina gave it to me to drop in your pigeon hole but I didn't see the need." Grace said handing a pink envelope to Ann. She had just returned to the room from her English class. Without hesitation she opened to see where it had come from. Inside she hoped it was from Kombo. She couldn't imagine that he could be so careless not to trace her after avoiding him that long. Could it be true that he had other women in his life and wouldn't care about losing her? She wondered how he could have pretended to be so in love with her if he didn't mean it? All these questions went through her mind as she struggled to open the letter. To her disappointment, it was not from Kombo. It was from Dr. Ayot informing her for a Women's conference at K.I.C.C in a week's time. She was required to prepare a paper on "Women's Marginalisation" for presentation at the conference.

"This is hectic," Ann said loudly.

"What is it Ann?" Grace asked perplexed by her reaction.

"Another assignment. Where does Ayot expect me to get time for these extra-curricular activities?" She said implying her reluctance to take up the assignment. "Anyway, I will do whatever I can, but for now, I have a Kiswahili tutorial assignment to work on. I have to meet my group members for a discussion." She said rising to leave. "See you later Grace. Take care of my visitors." She picked her folder and left.

"Good evening ladies!" Ann greeted her friends who had gathered in Jane's room for the discussion.

"Good evening to you Ann. But you are late," they responded unanimously. "Please sit over there." Rina directed her to sit on her bed because the available seats were already occupied.

"Okay girls. I apologise for being late. Where do we start?" Ann said trying to cheer up her friends.

"Anywhere." Alexandria replied. "But forgive me. Dan sent me to call you yesterday afternoon but I couldn't make it. I met a friend on the way who cornered me into taking another direction."

"Thanks for the message though it has been overtaken by events. Let's get to business." Ann said evasively trying to avoid talking about Dan. He was the last person she would have wished to think of at the moment.

After the discussion Jane offered them a cup of coffee. Ann would have preferred to leave immediately because she felt uneasy in the presence of Rina and Alexandria who she suspected to be her rivals over Kombo. She suspected that they were aware of her relationship with Kombo too and wished to avoid any incident that could lead to confrontation and embarrassment. However leaving earlier would imply uneasiness and increase suspicion, she thought. The wisest option therefore was to stay for a while and take the cup of coffee offered.

While her colleagues chatted over coffee, Ann sipped hers quietly trying to scheme in her mind the approach to Dr. Ayot's assignment.

"You are too quiet tonight. What is up?" Alexandria asked."

"Nothing really. Just thinking about the many assignments I have to accomplish." Ann replied politely.

"Oh, whose assignments? I hope not Dan's. Nowadays he appears very interested in you. Every time he talks of comparing his notes with yours, we always wonder what type of notes he's talking about. Take care. He's not a good man." Rina said as if giving advice.

"Sure, Why?" Ann asked as if interested in her friend's counsel. "You are asking why?" Alexandria intervened. "The guy is smart with women in this campus. I would do anything to catch his attention but he appears to fall for big brains like yours. I wish I was half as bright as you Ann."

The conversation was heading exactly where she did not want it to go. "God, please intervene and stop this madness," she prayed silently. "Hold your horses girls. Don't burn out for Kombo. He is a dangerous man," Rina said trying to calm their rising tempers. "Dangerous?" Everyone exclaimed surprised by the comment. "Come on Rina. You must be jealousy." Alexandria protested.

"Jealousy? No." Jane spoke for the first time. "I support Rina. That man is dangerous." She tried to stress her conviction over Rina's remarks.

"I was a victim Alexy. I can't blame you. I know he's a crafty man and above all, he has a soft spot for women. He never passes any but he is never serious either. Let me tell you ladies out of experience. When old Kombo falls for a woman, he falls with a bang. In most cases it is the victim to find her way out. I had to when I fell in his trap. I was three months pregnant when I established that he was married."

"Oh God! What did you do?"

Rina asked. "You ask me that. I did the most obvious. I flushed." "Flushed?" Ann asked jumping to her feet. "How did he react?" "I don't know." Jane replied. "What mattered to me then was how to get out of the problem. "Flushing was the best solution for me."

Shocked by what she had just heard, Ann felt strength departing from her body. She hadn't bothered to take precaution on her dates with him and anything was possible. Having enough reasons to drop

Kombo, she excused herself to leave but was forced to stay for a while to respond to Alexandria's question. She had wanted to know if Ann believed in the concept of "love."

"Ann, you are so indifferent please say something. Do you believe in love?" She repeated the question.

"Love, to me is like a toy a child gets on Christmas day or its birthday. The child can't leave it alone but sooner or later, the wheels come off and it is abandoned at the corner; never to bother its owner again." Ann explained figuratively.

"Why do you think so Ann"? Rina asked perplexed by her definition.

"Because to me, being in love means making another person the centre of your life and when that no longer exists, it is not love anymore. It is basically an unfair, unstable and paranoid relationship. I don't think I have time to waste on something like that. Love is like sex. Once you get to the peak, you start losing interest."

"But Ann!" Rina protested. "You are trying to generalise things. It is wrong to view relationship from that angle because we have stable marriages based on true love. Using the example of social misfits like Dan to discredit an essential concept like love is wrong."

"Marriage is a commitment that can exist on understanding even where love is dead." Ann snapped. She knew that her stand was radical and difficult to be understood by married women like Rina. To avoid unnecessary disagreement on the topic, she excused herself and left.

On the way to her hostel Ann thought about how wrong she had been about Dan. She had to do everything possible to avoid him. She felt hatred building at the revelation that he was a married man.

As she lay in bed that evening, Ann wondered if choosing to avoid him was the right thing. Deep within her, she still felt she loved him and was convinced that he loved her too even if it was for fun as perceived by her friends. She even wondered why she kept on arguing that love did not exist. If it didn't, what was she going through? Could it just be fascination from her inexperience or illusion? She asked herself over and over without finding a reasonable answer.

If she continued avoiding him, she thought, there would be a possibility of him giving up but wasn't it fair to confront him and let him know what she felt about him now? One thing she could not doubt was that there was something about him, which made him stand above other men she had met. It was something indefinite. She felt drawn to him as if by a magnet and even when her common sense urged her to back off, there was another part of her, which urged her to do exactly the opposite. This made her efforts to sort herself out futile.

*Captive of Fate*

# CHAPTER THIRTEEN

Ann's holidays were short. Two weeks for her was shorter than she would have wished. On her way to the bus stage she wondered what Kombo had been doing without her during this period.

As she made for the back seat in the bus, she noticed a familiar face which attracted her attention. "Who is she? And where did we meet?" she asked herself. Determined to remember where she had met this stranger, she resolved to sit on the opposite seat on the third row from the back. The other lady also indicated interest in Ann and smiled. "Hey Ann!" she greeted her.

"Oh, hey." Ann replied surprised by the realisation that the stranger knew her name.

"It's been a long time. Do you remember me?" The stranger asked.

"Oh, No! Where did we meet?" Ann exclaimed.

"We were together at Matungu. You were the assistant headgirl, if I am not wrong. But I was in form six when you were in fourth form", she tried to make Ann remember.

"Oh God!" Ann recalled. "You are Roxy the school Captain. I should have recalled that in the first place. Where are you nowadays?" Ann asked excited by the re-union.

"At Rift Valley University. I am in the final year. And you?" she asked.

"K.I.U" Ann replied. "Sure; then you know my husband; Mr. Kombo, he is a lecturer in the History Department".

"Oh, No!" Ann exclaimed. "You mean Dan is married?" she asked unconsciously drawing Roxy's attention.

"Why Ann?" she asked perplexed by her expression.

"Don't mind", she said as she tried to hide her disappointment. "It's…." she stammered looking for the right explanation. "It is just that some lady in our class was claiming to be engaged to the guy. You remember Adelite?" she lied implicating another lady in her class whom they had been together at Matungu.

"Yes, we come from the same village and she knows very well that Dan's my husband. She must be crazy." Roxy looked upset and Ann began to enjoy the scene. Kombo had to pay for lying to her, and in what better way than to hurt his wife enough to mess up their marriage if it ever existed. She thought quietly and bitterly at the realisation that Kombo was taking her for a ride.

Adelite appeared to be fond of Dan but that never implied a relationship. Ann thought. "Anything is possible," she assured herself. Roxy sunk into silence, obviously upset by Ann's revelations.

"The poor girl must be dying to get to Dan and clear the air over the matter!" Ann thought with a smile and resolved to leave her alone.

Back in college, life went back to normal. Being the final semester, she had to work extra hard to make up for the lost time within the remaining period.

For almost two hours Ann worked steadily on her assignments. The work occupied her mind completely. She had just succeeded in shutting out her painful thoughts when she heard a knock.

"Come in!" she shouted without looking up. The door opened almost instantly and when she looked up, it was Kombo.

"What are you doing here?" she asked nervously. Kombo laughed sarcastically and walked towards her.

"Is that the way to welcome me after we've been separated from each other for such a long time?" He said coming even closer.

"Dan No!" she cried anxiously leaping to her feet and moving a little out of his reach when she sensed that he was about to kiss her.

"What is the matter with you, Ann?" He demanded tersely. "You have been acting strangely since you reported back. Several times you have intentionally avoided me whenever we met accidentally. Why?" He demanded.

"You are imagining things," she lied.

"Am I?" he remarked cynically. "What happened during the holidays? Did you find another man? Or what the hell happened?" He asked after a frightening little silence.

"Yes you!" she wanted to shout at him but how could she do so without revealing her feelings in the process. She had to create a lie, and this she hated so much.

"No I didn't find another man. I haven't changed either."

"Sure." She could almost feel the cynicism exuding from him. His fist crashed down on her table making her jump with fright. "Damn you Ann! What is the matter with you?" he shouted at her. "You've blown hot and cold on me and I demand to know why?"

"If you want to know, then I will tell you." She shouted back at him resorting to anger in this moment of stress. But she could not tell him the actual truth. "I think it's time our...our relationship ended and I stand by what I told you initially. I don't want to be involved with you."

"So you don't want to be involved as you said before, do you?" his taunting voice penetrated her tired mind. "Tell me now, how you are going to accomplish that feat when you have already involved yourself so deeply."

While she listened to his words, she sobbed convulsively for she could no longer repress what she was feeling. She was obliged to yield. She felt shaken from head to toe with acute distress. When she did speak, it was only to express an impetuous wish that she had never been born and never have met him.

"Because you hate me!" he said. The vehemence of emotion, stirred by grief and love within her was claiming mastery and struggling for full sway, assuring a right to predominate, to overcome, to live and reign at last. Finally, she responded.

"I grieve at the thought of giving you up. For sure, I love you. I have cherished every moment we spend together. In your presence I feel so free. I haven't been buried with inferior thoughts. I have talked to you with what I reverence; delight in and with an original, vigorous and open mind. Sir, it strikes me with terror and anguish to feel I must be torn from you forever. Nevertheless, I still see the necessity of giving you up."

"Where do you see the necessity?" he asked suddenly.

"You ask me where? That's unfair." She replied.

"Okay, in what shape?" he persisted.

"In the shape of Roxana, your sweet wife."

"My wife!" he exclaimed shocked by the realisation that she knew about Roxy. "Ann! I have told you over and over again that I don't have a wife. I desperately need one whom I have now found. It is you dear. Please believe me!" he implored.

"Believe you! That is a wrong word Dan!" she remarked. Realising that he was not ready to admit that he had a wife, she went on to explain to him how she had met Roxana and their conversation in the bus.

"What a coincidence God!" Dan thought feeling trapped in a web of circumstances that he wished should never have occurred. What would he say to convince her that he was not married to Roxana?

Ann expected him to say something but he couldn't. This made her feel more irritated. "You lied to me that she's your cousin Dan. Didn't you? Deny it now!"

When had he told her this? He tried to remember. "Oh! Yes" he now remembered. She had seen Roxana's photos in his album and the only logical explanation he could give then was that they were related. He should have known better that they could meet. He cursed himself. "It's true Ann," he finally admitted.

"Then! What do you expect me to do Kombo? Do you think I should ignore the reality and pretend that I don't care? Do you think that I can sit around to remain a nothing to you? Do you think that I am an automation? A machine without feelings eh!" She was roused to anger and questions came out involuntarily.

"Ann!" he called her in a low soft voice.

"You are misguided about this. Give me a chance to explain"

Ann was too angry to listen. "Kombo!" she burst out. I have feelings just as you do and a heart too. May be if God had gifted me with some beauty and a good background like your wife, things would be different. Do you think that because I am poor, obscure and plain, I am soulless and prone to misuse by privileged people like you?" she took a pause and stared at him helplessly.

Kombo remained quiet for a while thinking of what to say but Ann couldn't remain quiet. It was time to pour out her heart and she had to do it with all might.

"I think you have neither sympathy nor love for women." She snapped. "If you ever had respect for them you would never go around messing up people's daughters under the pretence of a single desperate man while you have a wife. I scorn such behaviour."

Pierced by these words, he grabbed her so violently that she feared he would crush her but instead he hugged her to his breast. Determined to fight on like a mutinying slave, Ann continued with her quarrel. "I think I am better off without a man if that is what marriage means. Let me go!" she struggled to disentangle herself from him.

"Where do you want to go Ann?" he asked.

"Anywhere away from you." He released her but did not move away.

"Ann, be reasonable," he pleaded. He pulled a chair and sat down facing her while she sat on the bed. They sat quietly for a while. In this silence, Ann broke into sobs. He sat looking at her quietly but seriously. For sometime she wept uncontrollably. Moved by her sobs, he pulled her to himself and remained silent as she wept over his shoulder. After a while, he lifted her in his arms and sat on the opposite bed, holding her on his lap like a baby.

She was his baby, he thought and he had hurt her so much that he didn't know what to do to restore her childlike confidence in him.

"Calm down dear!" he finally spoke. "It's only you I intend to marry. I want you for a wife because I don't have any now. I wish you gave me a chance to make this choice. I don't deny your allegations about Roxana because they are true to some extent. I carelessly got involved with her at one time and she has my baby but I can't marry her. I regret to confess this to you but I wish to assure you that without you in my life, everything will come to a standstill; even my career" He confessed.

Ann remained silent. She thought he was mocking her and despised him.

"Come on Ann, don't let Roxana stand between us. Perhaps if you give me time I will be able to explain myself better. You are the wife I want: my only choice. Ann, will you marry me?" he proposed. Ann could not answer him still. She writhed herself from his grasp for she was still incredulous.  Do you still doubt me dear?"

"Entirely!" she replied.

"Then you have no faith in me?" Kombo asked.

"Not a whit."

"I am a liar in your eyes!" he remarked passionately. Ann ignored the remark and remained silent but Kombo proceeded. "Little sceptic, you shall be convinced. Let me assure you that I am ready to take every pain to prove to you that you Ann, I must have for my own, entirely."

Ann thought he was crazy. She stole a glance at his face and was surprised. He looked very much agitated and frantic. His eyes had a strange gleam.

Realising that she was looking at him he spoke again. "Oh Ann, you torture me with that searching and yet faithful and generous look. Please have mercy."

"How can I do that if you are truthful and your offer is real? My only feelings to you would be gratitude and devotion. They could never be torture."

"Gratitude!" he exclaimed wildly standing on his feet. Imagining that she had reviewed her stand, he held her right hand with both hands and said, "Ann! Accept me quickly. Say Kombo I will marry you".

"Are you serious?" Ann asked. "Do you really mean it? Do you sincerely wish me to be your wife?" She asked seriously.

"I do. And if an oath is necessary, I will swear." Kombo said impatiently.

"But sir, what about Roxy and the baby?"

Ann's question got Kombo off- balance. He had hoped that Roxy's chapter was closed. But there she was revisiting the issue. What would he say? He asked himself before responding. "There are many reasons." Kombo said looking for the right words.

"Go on." Ann said ignoring his reluctance to proceed.

"Okay I will tell you," he said. "Roxy's feelings are centred on one thing; money. Without money, there's no life for her. Secondly, she is proud and that needs humbling. Finally she is irrationally conspicuous. I can't afford to maintain that kind of woman." He said this hoping that it would please Ann and make her feel more appreciated. Ann remained quiet for a while before responding.

"You have a curious designing mind Dan. I am afraid your principles on some areas are artificial."

"Not at all Ann. Never! My principles were never trained." He protested. "They have grown a little awry for want and attention."

"Sure?" she looked at him inquisitively.

"Yes I am sure"

Ann closed her eyes to think about Kombo. "I love this man. God knows I do. More than words have power to express" she thought silently remembering every happy moment they had shared.

Kombo noticed her absentmindedness and asked, "You look disturbed dear. What is it? Speak it. Don't let it eat you up. It breaks my heart to see you in that state."

"Nothing serious Dan." She smiled at him.

"Then tell me about it. Please do." Dan persisted.

"Okay I will say it. I...I will marry you Dan."

Kombo hardly believed what he had heard. Would it be possible for Ann to mean it after what he had put her through, he asked himself. And if she did, what would he do to keep her from knowing the remaining puzzles. He would have to ensure that it doesn't happen again.

"Sir, didn't you hear what I said? Or you are too suprised to believe it. Ann asked.

"Yes I did hear Ann, everything" he said. Overwhelmed with affection, he could not control his feelings anymore. He stood and beckoned her. "Come to me dear. I am dying for your warmth."

Ann stood and hugged him affectionately. For a while they stood quietly holding on to each other. And then Kombo spoke. "Ask me for anything dear. It is my delight to be entreated and to yield. Pardon me God. Let no man interfere. Let me have her forever." Ann laughed heartily pushing him away.

"Don't be crazy. Human beings don't live forever. Why can't we go for supper at the students' centre?"

"Sure. Why not?" I will be waiting down in the car. Please hurry up." He kissed her lightly on the cheek and left.

# CHAPTER FOURTEEN

Ann got bored with the book she had been reading and closed it. She yawned loudly and looked at her watch. It was six o'clock. "Oh God, I can't believe I have been reading for two hours. "I should be going crazy." She said as she stood to gather her belongings. "Sophie!" she called her friend who was sitting opposite her on the reading table. Sophie appeared absorbed in her book and would have ignored Ann's disturbance if she hadn't persisted. "Sophie!" she repeated loudly. "Stop ignoring me. I know you are."

Sophie closed her book and looked at Ann. She was annoyed by her mischief but she knew that Ann would never give up. "What is it Ann?" she asked.

"Nothing" Ann replied. "Don't you think that you've read enough for the day? Mark you today is Friday, and the last thing I expect from you is to stick around for the evening. You need a break to freshen up dear. Let's go for dinner." Ann insisted.

"Okay, if you think so." Sophie replied indicating the will to leave. But before she stood up, she asked Ann what she intended to do after dinner.

"To go out. Ann replied suspecting a naughty thought from Sophie.

"Where in particular?" Sophie insisted.

"Somewhere with someone special."

Sophie knew that the only special person in Ann's life was Kombo. She resented the idea and had taken pain to try and introduce Ann to her cousin whom she knew was honest and trustworthy but she hadn't shown any interest. "Try to be specific Ann. You don't have to keep secrets from me. We are friends. Aren't we? Who is this special person?" Sophie demanded.

"Kombo, as usual." Ann replied.

"Gracious God!" Sophie sneered. "You with that toad! When will you come to your senses and drop that old man. He is old enough to be your grandfather Ann. Give him up. He is an embarrassment. I wish you took time to know Henry. He's the right guy for you."

"Stop it!" Ann shouted drawing the attention of other students.

"May-be we should talk from outside." Sophie remarked embarrassed by the incident. She pushed her chair back and made for the door.

Ann felt embarrassed too and blamed Sophie for being stubborn. She was angry at Sophie's resentment for Kombo but shouting at her in the Library was the last thing she should have done. She also pushed her chair back and followed Sophie hoping to sort out the misunderstanding outside the Library.

Sophie didn't stop to wait for her. She left straight for the hostel and had no intention of talking to Ann. Ann followed her almost running to catch up but Sophie did not bother to look behind.

"Sophie!" she shouted as she approached her.

"What is wrong with you Ann?" Sophie asked as she stopped, irritated by the realisation that Ann had followed her. "What do you want from me. You should be chasing after Kombo; not me" she said sarcastically.

"Look here Sophie!" Ann said as she caught up with her. "Whatever I do with Kombo should not bother you. I am old enough to choose what is best for me. I do not despise your cousin but I do not feel for him what I feel for Kombo. You should allow me time to sort out my feelings for the two men independently. Please understand." She pleaded with Sophie who appeared disinterested in the explanation.

"You don't have to explain to me anything Ann. Do what you think is best for you. I don't think I want to interfere anymore. That is why I want you to leave me alone for now. I am sorry I can't go with you for dinner. I have to go home. Bye Ann." She said and took off.

Ann stood confused for a while; not sure of how to interpret Sophie's reaction. "To hell with her !" She resolved with a sigh to skip dinner at the campus and have it at Kombo's.

As she stood outside Kombo's door, Ann wondered where he was. She had knocked several times without getting any response and was sure he was out. "But where?" She asked herself. She had called his office before coming to the house and he wasn't there either. Wherever he was, she resolved to wait for him at the house. She had a key to the house and would wait the whole weekend if he failed to turn up.

She unlocked the door and got in quickly because it was cold and dark outside. When she switched on the light, she saw a note on the table which drew her attention. Driven by instinct, She picked it up to read the contents hoping it was Dan's but to her surprise, the handwriting looked strangely familiar. "God! This is impossible." Ann exclaimed when she established that the note was from Adelite. "So these two are actually friends," she said loudly remembering her conversation with Roxana when she had implicated Adelite to avoid being suspected. In the note, she had requested Dan to pick her at Juja Junction at 7.30 p.m. Ann checked her watch to confirm the time out of curiosity. It was actually 7.40 p.m

She didn't want to believe what was happening. The thought of Kombo with another woman was unbearable. Why did he continue hurting her if he really cared for her? She wondered. Struck by disappointment she felt strength departing from her body. She pulled a chair and sat at the dining table feeling angry and miserable. She remembered Sophie's counsel and wished she had believed her. May be Sophie had been right. Henry appeared more honest and serious. But how could she trust him? He was a man like Kombo and of high class too, Ann thought.

Tears burnt her eyes. She was almost choked with fury. She wanted to cry and she had to. She wept to her exhaustion. She should have fallen asleep in the course of her weeping. When she woke up after a while, she felt a strong headache. The pain was so much that she could barely see. Struggling to her feet, she staggered to the bedroom and checked in the bedside drawer for painkillers. "Thank God they are there," She said as she picked a pink envelope with a label 'Panadol' on top. In the kitchen, she found dishes in the sink; dirty and stinking as if they had been there for a week. Ann felt dizzy and feared she would faint. Without wasting time, she steadied herself on the sink, swallowed the tablets and drank water from the tap using her bare hands. She then went back to the bedroom and lay on the bed to rest until her headache subsided.

When Ann woke up, Kombo was still out. She looked at the wall clock to confirm the time and noticed that it was ten in the night. Where could Dan be at such an odd hour of the night? Was it possible that he had decided to spend the night out with Adelite without bothering to inform her? And was it necessary to hurt herself over a careless man like Dan? Ann tried to convince herself that she had done the right thing. How could she know that Kombo was a crook without setting him up? "May-be it is high time I did the same to him. He may as well realise that I am not as naïve and innocent as he thinks." She thought as she sat up in bed and resolved to call Henry. She had his house telephone contact and would use Kombo's telephone which she realised was unlocked.

"Hello!" A female voice responded from the other end. Ann hesitated to pursue the call. Who could she be and what was she doing in Henry Odipo's house at 10.30 p.m? Could it be that Henry was engaged or even married?" Ann asked herself unsure of whether she had done the right thing to call at such time.

"Hallo! Is somebody on the line?" the lady in Odipo's house inquired impatiently.

"Oh…Yes. May I speak to Mr. Odipo please" Ann gathered strength and replied. After her disappointment with Dan, she didn't mind creating trouble for any man. May-be Odipo was married too. She thought.

"May I know who is calling please" The lady insisted.

"My name is Ann. I have some urgent information for him please".

Sophie wondered if it was Ann calling. How could she do that after the quarrel at K.I.U and what she had said about Henry? She had openly confessed her stand over Henry and it was unfair for her to play with his attention. To confirm her curiosity, she had to inquire from the caller.

"Is that Ann Maloba of K.I.U?"

Ann felt surprised at the question. She could hardly think that Sophie was at Henry's place. "May-be she is" she thought and resolved to ask. "Is that Sophie?"

"Of course, you witch, where are you calling from? I hope not at Kombo's." Sophie teased her.

Ann felt angry at the memory of Dan and did not wish to discuss anything to that effect with Sophie.

"Sophie Please!" she pretended to be impatient. "Don't start stories. We will talk later. Let me talk to Henry please."

"If you insist; yes. Just hold on for a minute. He's in bed. Henry! There's special call for you. Please hurry up" Sophie shouted.

"Who is it", Henry asked. Ann could hear his voice clearly over the phone.

"Guess who? It's Ann." Sophie answered. "Hallo!" a male voice came on the line.

"Hello!" she said nervously not sure of what to tell him. She felt excited listening to his soothing voice but was confused about what to tell him. When she picked up the phone to call him, it was out of disappointment from Dan. She had even hoped to miss him. But there he was on the line. What would she say? She stood and paced around the table trying to frame something in her blank mind.

"Hello Ann! Are you still there?" Odipo sounded curious.

"Oh Yes. How are you doing? Please forgive me for calling this late. It's just that..." she ran out of words again. She began to realise that what she was saying could hardly make sense.

Henry noticed that she had run out of words. He had to save
her from the embarrassment;

"It's okay Ann. You don't have to apologise, please feel free to call
me anytime you feel like. It is my pleasure to hear that sweet voice
especially now. How are you?" Odipo teased her.

"Fine!" she replied and that's all she could say.

"That's great." Henry said after a short while. "You must be
enjoying yourself this being a Friday. Who is the lucky guy with
you? I envy him." He teased her again trying to provoke her into a
conversation.

"Oh No! Don't tell me you are that jealous." Ann finally found
confidence to talk.

"You don't have to feel threatened. I am alone in college. In
fact I got bored with books and the best way to rid off the boredom
is to talk to someone special like you. Does that satisfy your
curiosity?" She lied determined to impress him as a good girl.

"So, what can I do for you now?" he asked.

"Nothing much. A wish for a good night will do." Ann felt
relaxed now and all she needed was a good sleep. She wished Kombo
would spend the night out so that she could have a peaceful night.

"I don't think that's the best idea.  What about spending the
night here? I could pick you up in an hour's time" Odipo said
encouragingly.

"Please no. You don't have to do that. I am fine here." Ann
protested but Odipo seemed determined.

"I wouldn't mind if you did Ann. But if you insist, I will withdraw
my offer on condition that you assure  me when I can see you
soonest.

"That's okay with me" Ann replied. What about tomorrow
afternoon? I need to study in the morning hours and then you can
pick me up at around 2pm. But this should be at your convenience."
She stressed. She would have loved to spend the night at Henry's
but it was not possible because she was stuck at Dan's house.

"That is okay with me too. Then let me wish you a good night as you said."

"Good night Henry. See you tomorrow." Ann said and replaced the receiver.

When she sat down to think about the next day, she felt hungry. It's then that she realised that she hadn't had dinner. She had been too angry with Kombo to feel hungry. But with Henry on her mind now, she resolved to go to the kitchen and prepare dinner for herself even if it was very late.

*Captive of Fate*

# CHAPTER FIFTEEN

Beaming, Ann walked into her room carrying a paper bag full of delicacies. "Hey Faith" she greeted her roommate who was reading a Bible.

"Hey Ann. You look marvellous. What's the catch?" Faith asked knowing that Ann could hardly afford that kind of shopping.

"Don't mind. Things are getting better." She replied and proceeded to unpack. "These are yours" she handed Faith a packet of biscuits and passion juice.

"Thank you Ann. It's kind of you." Faith said as she stood to receive the items. Ann continued to unpack hers and arranged them in the sideboard beside her bed. As she picked the pillow to straighten her bed, she saw a blue envelope, which had been under the pillow. Faith noticed the surprise on her face as she opened the envelope.

"Adelite gave me that letter to pass to you but I forgot. I am very sorry." Faith tried to explain.

The name Adelite made her feel dizzy. She wondered how a woman could be involved with a man romantically and still be used as a go-between, between him and another woman.

"Shameless slut." She thought as she read through Dan's note. He was inviting her to Dinner at his house. "Shameless bastard" she said loudly drawing Faith's attention.

"Who is the bastard Ann?" Faith asked after noticing that she was angry with what she had just read.

"Don't mind. I will prove to him that I am not as stupid as he thinks." She tore the note into pieces.

"Who is he?" Faith insisted.

"I will tell you later. I have to leave for town immediately."

"Again?" Faith exclaimed perplexed by the fact that Ann had just arrived from town and it was already 6.30 p.m.

"Don't worry Faith. I will take care of myself. See you in the morning." She said locking up her wardrobe and left. She hadn't even changed her clothes.

"Whatever it is she is up to, only God knows" Faith remarked with a sigh and continued reading her Bible.

On her way to Kombo's house, Ann thought about Henry. Remembering their afternoon together, she wished they had stayed longer. They had started it at his house discussing topical and political issues and then proceeded to a hotel where they had snacks before they went to the supermarket. At the supermarket he had told her to pick anything she wanted and thereafter dropped her at the college without making any passes to indicate that he was interested in her sexually. In her perception, Henry, was a mature and responsible man although he looked younger than Dan in age. Dan was a careless romantic and all she saw in his eyes was lust. Could it be true that Sophie had been right all along when she recommended Henry as the right candidate? She asked herself.

For the first time Ann thought about marriage seriously. What kind of husband could she go for? What would be her expectations of him? At this point, she began to realise that she had made a mistake by promising to marry Dan. She had entered a marriage commitment without considering possible consequences.

Dan's house was a kilometre away from the bus stage. Since she alighted in the early evening darkness, she ran to keep pace with other commuters headed for the same direction for company and security reasons. As she stood outside Dan's door, Ann wondered if it was proper meeting Kombo at his house where she was vulnerable to his harassment. For five minutes, she stood quietly debating whether she should go a head and knock or turn back. Inside, she felt angry and almost hated him except that she was yet to prove if he had actually been out with Adelite. It was wrong to speculate instead of seeking confirmation. She thought as she proceeded to knock the door.

The evening did not progress quite as she had imagined it would. Ann found herself staring with mixed feelings at the man seated opposite her and endlessly had to remind herself of his treachery when her yearn for him appeared to over-rule her deep seated anger. The forcefulness of his strong personality was etched deeply in her heart and mind, and she wondered how she could have forgotten his existence so completely over the past days.

Piercing eyes probed her shuttered glance and a frown appeared between the heavy brows. "Is something troubling you Ann?" Dan asked.

"Why should there be something troubling me?" she responded with forced casualness.

"You have been very quiet this evening, almost pre-occupied." His hand found hers across the table and that familiar current of awareness passed through her as he leaned towards her enviously.

"You are not feeling ill, are you?"

"No" she shook her head, trying to weigh whether his concern was genuine or part of his acting. "I have never felt better," she added with a hint of flippancy in her voice.

He released her hand and leaned back in his chair to observe with a brooding expression on his face. His rapier sharp eyes travelled from her new hair style down to the seductive hollow between her breasts before they swept upwards to her face once more as if searching for something. "You are different, somehow," he admitted at last and she smiled inwardly with cynical satisfaction. "Yes, I feel different". She admitted with care.

His glance sharpened perceptibly. "Something happened to make you feel this way!"

"One could say so, yes." She said, bitterness curling her usually soft lips.

"Want to tell me about it?" he asked, his eyes watchful.

"Later perhaps." she waved aside the subject. "I am sure there's something you wanted to discuss with me."

"That can wait as well," he said with an odd almost haunted expression in his eyes. "More coffee?" Ann asked.

"No, thank you" his mouth tightened animously. "Shall we go then?"

"Where?" she asked fully conscious of his intention

"To bed."

"Now! The answer is no. If you have nothing else to tell me, drop me at college."

Ignoring her remarks, he rose and walked over to her side. She saw his face kindled and his eyes flashing with tenderness and passion in every lineament. She quizzed momentarily, then rallied. A weapon of defence had to be prepared. She withheld her tongue but as he reached for her, she asked. "Who do you intend to marry between me and Adelite?" As if electrocuted, he stepped back instantly. How had she learnt of his affair with Adelite? He asked himself. Could it be that he had under estimated her? First Roxy, and then Adelite. Who would be next to be found out! he wondered.

"Answer me Dan." Ann demanded impatiently.

"What do you mean? Which Adelite?" he asked confused by the trend of events. Without further questions, she opened her purse, picked Adelite's note and handed it to him.

Dan felt angry; not with Ann or Adelite but himself. Ann noticed his state of confusion and wondered. She had never seen him in such a fury before. He looked scary and she had to take refuge somewhere, anywhere away from him. Noticing that the visitor's room was open; she fled into it and shut the door behind her locking it up. With her back on the door, she let the burning tears in her eyes flow voluntarily until they were no more. Finally, she jumped into bed and tried to ignore him.

Dan's pleading outside got into her nerves. She couldn't bear it anymore. Why wouldn't he leave her alone? If he really cared for her as he pretended to, why did he continue dating other women? How could he be so careless? In the midst of these questions Ann broke into sobs.

"Ann! I never meant to wound you. My love for you is true. Please forgive me." Kombo banged the door once more.

Driven by fury, Ann jumped out of bed and opened the door. "How many times am I supposed to forgive you Dan?" she dashed out forcing Dan to retreat few steps back. She was too angry to care but when she looked at his face, she recoiled inside, wondering what sort of person Kombo was. There was such remorse in his eyes and pity on his face. Ann wanted to feel sorry for him but she couldn't. He had betrayed her trust. He didn't deserve any. She thought bitterly.

"You are disgusting Kombo" she said and went back to the table where the quarrel had started. Dan followed her and sat on the opposite chair across the table.

"What! Why?" he exclaimed hastily. "What disgusts you about me?"

"Everything. Your unfaithfulness Dan. What do you expect me to do? Thank you for cheating on me with my classmate?"

"Ann!" he stared at her helplessly. "Give me time; I will explain. But not now."

"It's okay. Ask for the time when you are ready to explain. As for now, you can as well forget that we were ever involved".

Kombo remained silent for a while. He appeared to be in deep thought. Ann chose to ignore him and think about her situation. Noticing her careless state, he resolved to explain himself out hoping she would change her attitude about his behaviour.

"You should be having a strange opinion of me. I can't blame you. You must regard me as a plotting profligate and a low rage who has been simulating disinterested love in order to draw you into a snare deliberately laid and strip you of your honour and rob you self respect." Ann knew that it was the plain truth. She however resolved to remain silent and let him dissect himself.

"I see. You can say nothing." He remarked. "In the first place you are still angry and have to struggle to draw your breath; secondly you can't yet accustom yourself to accuse and revile me because it is not your nature. Besides the floodgates of tears are open and tears would rush out if you spoke.

"Console yourself." She thought amused by his conclusions. They remained silent for a while before she finally spoke. "Everything has changed now; true relationships are based on trust and faithfulness. I can't trust you anymore. I think we should part ways."

"But why?" he demanded miserably.

"Because there're many others in your life. I can't afford to compete."

"Ann, you don't know what you are talking about." He laughed nervously. Adelite is not my type for a wife. She is too demanding."

"Stop it!" she shouted at him. "You have no right to speak ill of her. First it was Roxana and now Adelite. Who is next? Do you tell them the same about me? It's cruel to go around confusing people's daughters for selfish motives and later describe them with vindictive antipathy. What's wrong with you Dan? You must be a sadist." Ann was very angry with him. She wanted to scream but could not. She had to cover her mouth to avoid saying things that would make her regret.

"You misjudge me Ann." He protested. "What you are saying is a complete insult. It is not fair." He said suppressing the rising furry.

He stood up and paced around the room for a while before he walked over to her. Ann looked at him unmoved. "Look Ann," he bent over the table facing her directly. "This relationship has run smoothly enough so far but I always knew there would come a knot and puzzle. Here it is now for vexation and exasperation and endless trouble. For God's sake Ann, don't tempt me to use some force." He threatened her hoping that it would cool her down. Ann, hear my reason! Because if you don't, I will try violence." His voice turned hoarse and his look frightening. She realised that in another moment, and in one impetus of frenzy, he would lose control and she would be able to do nothing against him. She had very little time to sort out the situation because a movement of repulsion, a fight or struggle would seal her doom. What could she do?

Inside, she felt strong. She felt an inner power and a sense of influence which supported her. This crisis was perilous, but not without charm. Taking his clenched fist, she loosened the contorted fingers and spoke to him soothingly,

"Sit down. I will talk to you as long as you like and listen to all you have to say; whether reasonable or unreasonable"

He sat down and Ann felt relieved but could not get leave to speak directly. She felt caught up in a web that was almost unbearable. She struggled to suppress burning tears in her eyes with great pain to avoid breaking down before him but realised it wasn't possible. Finally she gave up and let them flow freely and as long as they wanted. If the flood annoyed him, so much the better. She gave way and cried heartily.

Kombo felt angry as he watched tears rolling down her cheeks. He was not angry with Ann but himself. How could he break the heart of a young trusting girl like Ann? She was too innocent to understand his unfaithfulness and whatever explanation he gave her could hardly be justified. He almost broke down himself when he realised the pain he was inflicting on her. She didn't deserve it, he thought and he had to do something to rectify the situation.

"I am sorry darling. I didn't know that it would end up like this. It's just that I love you so much that the frozen look on your little steeled face scared me. The thought of losing you drives me crazy Ann. Will you forgive me?" He asked softly.

His softened voice announced subduction and confirmed to Ann that he had calmed down. This gave her the feeling that she was out of danger and she relaxed, hoping the battle was over. He made an effort to touch her hand but she pulled it away before he could reach it. He should have mistaken her calmness to yielding to his dirty tricks but he was wrong. "Ann! Ann!" He called her in such a tone of bitter sadness that it thrilled along every nerve she had. "Don't you love me anymore? Why do you recoil from my touch as if I was some Ape or Lion."

"You are both Dan" she thought reassuringly but could not dare to speak aloud. She felt tortured by his behaviour so much that she would have shot him if she had a gun. She had to talk to him anyway, she resolved even if it meant framing her message in a way that was less provoking.

"I do love you more than I can explain but I cannot indulge the feeling. One thing I know is that there's no possibility of a future between us. At least not after what I know about you," she paused to let him respond to her conclusion.

Kombo appeared absent minded and stayed for a while before bursting out. He was obviously violent again. "Look Ann, you should blot out of your mind the idea of leaving me. God knows you are the centre of my life and I will never rest until I get you." He stood, walked over to Ann and stared at her face sternly.

"You will be my wife both virtually and normally. You may go places or even marry another man but it will only be temporary. You will still come back to me because God's will must be done." His voice and hands quivered. His eyes blazed scaring Ann out of her skin again but it only inspired her to fight on.

"He must be crazy," she thought bitterly. She wasn't going to give in for whatever reason because she was at least convinced that he was insane.

"Sir!" She spoke calmly. "One thing I am convinced of is that marrying you is accepting to be a mistress. Your taste for women appears unlimited and your lust, insatiable. I don't think I want to commit my life to a man of that nature. How many?..."

"Ann!" He shouted at her unable to endure her words. "Ann! I am not a good-tempered man. You forget that. Neither am I long enduring. I am not cool and dispassionate. For your own good and for God's sake, stop insulting me. I know that you are angry and could be contemplating leaving me but give me some attention. I don't love being what I am Ann, God knows I am a victim of life's cruelty."

Ann laughed sarcastically. "Sure!" she exclaimed. "May be you should explain further. I would love to hear about the cruel past that turned you into that terrible nature."

"Ann please", he pleaded, agitated with fury. He held her shoulders and shook her violently but stopped suddenly as if stopped by someone. Tears welled up in his eyes as he moved away from her. Bending and holding on to the dining table, he broke into sobs. Ann barely caught his words as he mumbled amidst sobs."

"Oh God! What have I done to deserve this? Why must I suffer at the hands of women? What a terrible curse! But God, don't let this one escape. Please he broke into louder sobs again."

Ann felt terrified. She couldn't endure this state anymore. It was embarrassing and out of control. She wanted to cry too but of what use could her crying be to an insane mind? She had to do something again. She thought.

"Please calm down," she implored. She took his hand and led him to the nearby chair. "Please sit down and tell me about your past. It might help to sort out this mess" she squeezed his hand and forced a smile hoping that it would soothe him up. The trick worked. He gradually calmed down and managed to compose himself again. Assured of his recovery she led him on gently.

"Tell me about it darling. I am listening."

"It's okay Ann. Whatever happened in the past and what has happened now is somehow out of my control. I can't blame you. I blame fate."

"Tell me about this fate Dan." She said encouragingly.

"If you give me chance, I will explain."

"Please do. I really pity you."

"Pity! Ann, from some people to me is noxious and insulting. But yours is different. I can read it in your face. It's like that of a suffering mother. I accept it. And I know you can help me. Okay, I will tell you everything. I was engaged to a lady called Hellen. I loved her and was convinced she would be my wife but fate struck."

"What happened? Did she die?" Ann interrupted.

"No, two weeks to my introduction meeting with her parents, Hellen eloped with a banker. I was heartbroken, but there was nothing I could do."

"Oh God! That was unfair. How did you get yourself out of the mess?"

"I despaired Ann. A remnant of self-respect was all that intervened. In the eyes of my friends and relatives I was without any doubt a failure and covered with shame. To try and forget her, I resorted to chasing companionship from women. My profession gave me, access to variety of them; both students and working class. But none seemed to satisfy me. Ann, can you believe that?"

Ann was keenly following his story. It sounded pathetic and she sympathised with his situation. But she could not find any grounds to justify his behaviour.

He looked at Ann desperately expecting a positive response but she didn't seem to view the situation from his angle.

"No, I don't believe that. Whatever you did after losing Hellen is unforgivable. Why did you have to transfer your vengeance to innocent women? How many of them do you think trusted you and ended up heart broken? Assume it was your sister or daughter Dan, how would you feel? Didn't your conscience haunt you after every incident?"

"Not at all in the true sense. I was determined and convinced that I ought to. It was not my original intention to hurt anybody. As I told you, my passion for women was uncontrollable but short-lived. "And mine is too." Ann exclaimed

"No. Yours is different. It is real, very true." He responded quickly looking at her face as if in appeal. "Ann, believe me. You seem to doubt my confession. I can swear. For sure, I have no intention of cheating on you. But I occasionally lose control and that you should understand. It doesn't mean that I despise you. Can you accept me the way I am dear?" He looked at her expectantly but Ann remained quiet.

"You perplex me Ann. You look at me as if you are not satisfied with my testimony. Why?"

"Well what my look implies is that I expect you to continue. Is that all you had?" she asked casually.

"What else do you want to hear Ann?"

"I can't actually tell. Eh… Did you ask any of them to marry you?" she asked.

"Sure". Kombo sighed. "About three years back, I met a first year student who attracted me. She was slender, dark skinned and beautiful in her unique way. She looked naive and innocent in many dimensions. Out of this fascination, I proposed marriage to her even after establishing that she had a baby. I assured her that I would adopt her son and she accepted but a year later she informed me that she had changed her mind about our commitment and resolved to reconcile with her son's father."

"How did you react to that?" Ann asked curiously.

"Oh! What do you think I could have done? I picked another lady to help me forget."

"Who was she? Another student?" Ann asked.

"No. She was a secretary in our department. I picked on her because she was readily available when I needed a distraction from Jane. I was also disillusioned about commitment and all I needed was a mistress with no strings attached. Nevertheless, we didn't go far."

"What happened? Ann interrupted.

"I met Cinta. She was unprincipled but strong headed and violent. Nonetheless she was beautiful and tempting."

"And then!" Ann interrupted again angry with his endless narrative of sexual encounters."

"And then what Ann? We broke up a few months later when she met Roxana at my house. But don't think that I am an unfeeling, loose-principled rake. I can read it on your face" he said defensively but Ann couldn't restrain her fury any more.

"That's what you are Dan. A loose-principled immoral sadist." She repeated his words as she stood up and pushed her chair back as if intending to leave. "Did it seem to you in the least wrong to live like that with the AIDS scourge around?"

"It did and let me assure you that I never liked what I was doing. It was a grovelling fashion of existence and I don't wish to return to it. You can help me stop it Ann. He also stood up and walked over to where Ann was standing. He wanted to hug her but she pulled away.

"Stop it Dan. Don't touch me you vile creature." She moved to the other side of the table where she stood facing Kombo once more. Kombo looked at her disbelievingly unable to judge her reaction. He had expected sympathy but he was receiving repulsion.

As she looked at him blankly, Ann felt the truth of those words and drew from them certain influences. If she were so far to forget herself and all the lessons that had been instilled in her under any pretext, she thought deeply, with any justification or through any temptation to become the successor of those poor girls and ladies, he would one day regard her with the same feelings which now in his mind deserted their memory. It was enough to feel it. She impressed it upon her heart that it might remain there to serve her as aide in the time of trial.

"Ann!" Kombo spoke after a while. "You are looking grave. You disapprove me still but let me tell you the truth. When I found you not long ago, I found you perfectly a new character. Your personality inspired me to explore you intimately. I had to search you deeper and know you better. In the course I met you full of strange contrasts."

"For example?" Ann interrupted.

"For instance your garb and manners are restricted to rule. Your air is often different and all together that of one refined by nature but absolutely unused to society and for a good deal afraid of making yourself disadvantageously conspicuous by some solecism. When addressed you lift a keen and glowing eye to your interlocutor's face, which has penetration and power in each glance. When plied by close questions you have ready and precise answers."

"Stop it!" Ann shouted. She was experiencing an ordeal. A hand of fury grasped her vitals. It was a terrible moment for her, full of struggle, darkness and burning rage. No human being could wish to be loved better than she appeared to be loved and worshipped by the monster before her. She had to renounce such an idolising love that had no basis as was portrayed in his behaviour. The nature of his love was unsteady and irresponsible. She had to leave him.

"Sir!" she finally spoke. "I have listened to your life's horrors and felt touched by every experience but that does not solve your puzzle. She wiped away some tears from her eyes. The conversation was becoming torture and had complicated everything. Her purpose of going to see him was to sort out the mystery surrounding his involvement with Adelite but he had avoided the topic from the start. She looked at her watch and noticed that it was 5 in the morning. She could hardly understand how the night had passed by without her knowledge. She hadn't even had dinner and began to feel weak.

"Ann! You are right. My history should not determine your judgement of me. Sure! Why dwell in the past when the present is sure and the future much brighter? I have found you and I believe you are God's choice for me. You are sympathetic and trustworthy, my angel and I am bound to you with strong attachment. I find you good, gifted and lovely." He moved and knelt before her.

"My attempts to hide the truth from you were out of fear; of the stubbornness that exists in your character. I feared early-instilled prejudice. I had to have you safe before hazarding confidentials. This was cowardly I admit. But now I have opened up to you plainly my life of agony, described to you my hunger and thirst for a higher and worthier existence and I now register my desire to live faithfully where I will faithfully be loved in return. Now I ask you to accept me as I am. Do it dear now!" he demanded.

Ann felt sick. "He must be insane," she thought bitterly.

"Ann! Just promise me that you will be mine and mine alone." He pleaded.

"And you! whose? Everybody's?" she said sarcastically.

"Ann, don't insult me." A wild look crossed his features. He rose but forbore yet. Ann retreated to the wall near the door and leaned on it for support. She shook with fear but stood resolved.

Kombo read her countenance and realised he was losing. His fury rose and he had to yield to it for a moment. He walked over to her and seized her arm. He then grasped her waist and devoured her with his flaming glance.

Physically, Ann felt powerless like dry grass exposed to a glow of furnace. But mentally she still possessed her strength and with it the certainty of ultimate safety. Instinctively her eyes rose to his and while she looked at the fierce face, she gave an involuntary sign. His grip was painful and her overtaxed strength almost exhausted.

"Never", he muttered, gritting his teeth. "Never has anything in my life been so frail though indomitable." He shook her with the force of his hold. "I could crash you like a louse between my nails. But what good will it do to me? I hate to consider that eye, resolute wild and that free thing looking out of it; defying me with more than courage. If I left my outrage loose and crashed you, a conqueror I might be but the inmate will escape to heaven before I posses it. Yet it is you; the spirit of will, energy, virtue and purity that I want. Ann! Come on and love me." He released her and staggered backward to the dinning table. His look was worse to resist than the frantic strain. Only an idiot could have succumbed now. She had dared and baffled his fury. She had to elude his sorrow.

Gathering the only strength left in her body, she dashed to the table and picked her purse. Kombo looked confused. Without hesitation, she walked to the door, opened it confidently and walked out.

"Are you going away Ann?" He asked, broken hearted.

"Yes sir, I have to."

"You won't come back to me? Why can't you be my rescuer and comforter? I know you're capable."

"Adelite will. Goodbye Dan. Farewell forever." She shouted as she descended the stairs into the early morning darkness.

*Captive of Fate*

# CHAPTER SIXTEEN

"There's one major reason why I love you. Take for instance the experiences you have gone through. The untiring assiduity with which you have persevered, the unflagging energy and the unshaken temper with which you have met difficulties make me acknowledge the compliment of the qualities I would want in a woman. I find you docile, diligent, sincere, consistent and courageous. With all these qualities, I am sure our life together would be complimentary. Believe me Ann I will try to restore meaning and happiness to your life if you give me the chance."

The speaker was Henry. After her ordeal with Kombo, he had generously provided her with a shoulder to cry on and in due course Ann had voluntarily disclosed her past without reservations. She found him gentle and understanding and after a few dates, she began to gain confidence and feel free in his presence. Henry enjoyed her child like faith in him and chose to hold up his feelings until she had built enough trust in him. He was a rich man and could easily buy her into his life but he didn't think it was the right thing to do for Ann. She was special and he wanted her for a wife not a mistress. Considering her past experience, money would never restore her confidence in men. She had suffered an enormous emotional trauma, which would require extreme emotional attention to heal. And that is what he was going to offer; undivided love and attention.

He was the owner of several magazines, two radio stations and a film and video production Company. He held a high profile in the media world but Ann had no idea. His "Millennium Communications" took up five floors on Highway Plaza with its head offices and advertising agency up but his personal office was on the ground floor.

He was thirty-five years old, nine years older than Ann. He had a physical toughness that made many people feel intimidated and this made his work easier. The harsh lines of maturity on his face made him look older than his real age. But this had more to do with his upbringing than his nature. As a school drop out at the age of fourteen, Henry had spent several years on the streets before finding his way into a job with a government media organisation which provided the basis for his advancement.

Ann wondered at how she had become fond of Henry. Was it a reaction to her break up with Kombo? She asked herself. How possible was it that he was laying ground for another disappointment? He had proved caring and responsible but was that all she would expect from a husband? These questions ran through her mind after Henry's proposal and made it impossible for her to make a conclusive decision. She barely knew his real character and he appeared secretive about his personal life. As wealthy as he appeared, it was hard to rule out the possibility of the existence of other women in his life. She wanted to ask him about it but she feared embarrassment. She didn't want him to think that she mistrusted him. But why did he propose to her then if he was in love with someone else? Would it be out of pity?

"Mr. Odipo" she finally spoke. "Your offer is too good to be true. I require time to think over it."

"It's true Ann. And if you require a whole month to think over it, I don't mind. I am always patient and if you have any doubts, please ask" he said looking at her reassuringly.

As they walked across the park towards his car, Ann thought about her past and her dreams. Was it possible that her dreams were beginning to be fulfilled? What else could she expect other than a loving, responsible and understanding man. She thought, embracing the vision of her marriage to Henry. May be it was an opportunity in her lifetime and the earlier she grabbed it, the better.

Henry felt disturbed about her too and as he walked besides her holding her hand, he wondered how her presence in his life had changed his perception of life. In his past he had met sophisticated and beautiful women who worshipped the grounds he walked on but none had impact on his feelings like Ann. She was a hard-bitten cynic like himself unsophisticated and undemandingly devoted. Such qualities could hardly exist in the sophisticated ladies he was dating and this had possibly contributed to his lack of interest in declaring a lifetime commitment like marriage to them. If only she knew how much he wanted her for a wife, he thought wishfully, she would have said yes to his offer without hesitation. He wanted her to be the mother of his children because she had all the qualities he expected from a perfect mother.

As they stood beside his car, he looked at her passionately and pulled her to himself. Ann felt his influence in her marrow and his hold on her limbs as she shivered with excitement. But her conscience still resisted. Kombo had capitalised on her emotional feelings to exploit her and she was determined to involve her head this time. Henry realised the confusion in her response and asked,

"Why are you reluctant to accept my proposal Ann?" I love you and all I want is confirmation that you are all mine. I can't stand the thought of losing you. Please reconsider…" He pleaded.

Ann stiffened at his words. They were exactly the same as those she had heard from Kombo on their first date. What a coincidence! She wondered.

"No Henry. It is not as simple as you think. This is a life time commitment and I just want to be sure that I am making the right decision. Please understand."

"I do understand Ann. But I have this burning feeling that in your state you need security and protection. And I can't give you that if I don't have you under my control." He said loudly almost becoming hysterical.

Ann felt angry at herself. Why did she have to cause so much anguish to respected men like Henry? She knew that he had the power and means to get better women and could not establish why he was hurting for a poor girl like herself. She had to do something to elude his pain.

"Henry, I think we should stop seeing each other for a while. We need time to sort out our feelings and…"

"Why Ann?" Henry interrupted. "Is it because I am ugly or I don't have a degree like you? What is it about me that disgust you. Please tell me." He shook her violently.

"Oh Henry," she looked at him helplessly blurting out the truth in her mind. "I love you so much more than I can admit, but I am confused especially after what happened between me and Kombo. I just can't trust any man yet." She said hot tears running down her cheeks.

"Okay Ann. Don't cry please." He handed her a handkerchief to wipe her tears.

"Thanks" she said trying to contain her grief.

"I am very sorry. I didn't mean to hurt you. Please forgive me," He said hugging her passionately. "I will wait. I think we should get going. It's getting late and I would like us to have dinner at my place. Sophie promised to fix one." He said opening the door for her to get in. Ann wanted to protest but resolved to succumb to his request for the sake of Sophie. She didn't want to disappoint her after the Kombo conflict.

When they were all safely seated in his car, he drove off to his house quietly. He knew her state of mind and thought the best thing to do was to let her ponder over her crisis without interfering. Beside him, Ann read well in his iron silence what he felt towards her. The disappointment of an austene and despotic nature, which had met resistance where it expected submission. She knew that as a man he would have wished to coerce her into submission but somehow he had failed to do so.

During dinner, Sophie tried to cheer them up but had little success. They all appeared to be in low spirit and the best she could do was to leave them alone.

Henry looked upset and hardly spoke to Ann except when asking for something. She found the situation very uncomfortable especially from a person she was trying to build confidence in. But remembering their argument at the park she had to understand his mood. She wished she could review her rigid stand and philosophical outlook about relationships to enable her socialise well with people. She barely tasted her food even when Sophie implored her. Henry finished his meal and walked to the study room without uttering a word. Ann felt worried because he had promised to drop her at the college after dinner. Looking at her watch she noticed that it was 8.30 pm and she could hardly make it to college on her own. It was risky and she knew Sophie wouldn't let her leave alone.

After the meal, she followed him to the study room and found him leaning on the shelf. He must have been in deep thought because he didn't notice her come in. Ann hated his mood of which she felt was due to her fault and wished she could reverse it.

"Henry, I am sorry about what transpired at the park. I have thought about it, and I truly feel sorry. Please forgive me." At first, he did not move. He just looked at her blankly from the head to her feet and then up again. He could be wondering what sort of person she was to follow him up and seek his attention after what had happened. She thought bitterly. Finally he spoke.

"It's okay. I have no grudge against you. After all you've been through, you have every reason to be careful and you are entitled to your own views too." He walked over to her and embraced her warmly. For a while, they stood locked up in the embrace without saying a word. Henry was the first to break the silence. "Let's get going" he said ushering her out of the door. You will be late."

*Captive of Fate*

# CHAPTER SEVENTEEN

If blushes are anything to go by, there's a lot you are not going to tell me." Sophie grinned. It was a hot afternoon and as they lay under a mango tree enjoying the cool breeze, Sophie noticed that Ann was not in her normal mood.

"Well," she said lamely, "some things are private." Sophie wanted her to say more but she didn't. She was feeling sad and depressed but she wouldn't disclose the cause to Sophie. It was improper because it had something to do with Henry; Sophie's favourite cousin. When she decided to move in and stay with Henry after her graduation, Ann thought it was the most reasonable thing to do as she had nowhere to stay in the city while she looked for a job. Besides, she had established that Odipo was a wealthy man with a multinational business and hoped she would be absorbed in one of its branches but she realised that she was wrong. His only interest in her was to make her a wife and while Sophie was working, he was busy making plans for their wedding. Ann's inquires over her employment were dismissed evasively to after the wedding. Furthermore, he had made it clear that he did not wish his wife to work. She thought about her dreams as a working class lady capable of improving her family's lifestyle and making lots of money to buy what she wanted. Would her dream ever come true if she succumbed to the marriage proposal? She thought seriously.

Sophie felt was not satisfied by her brief answer and wished she could say more. She stole a glance at her again and realised that she was looking miserable.

"Please Ann", she pleaded. "Tell me whatever is on your mind. You look so different. There's no more life on your face. In fact you have lost your glamour. Is something a miss Ann? Please don't hide it from me. I may be in a position to assist."

Ann took sometime to respond. She had been fighting inside on whether it was reasonable to tell Sophie the truth. In essence she felt responsible for her situation and thought she should face the consequences alone.

"I am sorry Sophie for the worries I am putting you through. I am actually in a fix which I feel personally responsible and the thought of how to get out makes me feel so helpless and miserable".

What is it! Come on Ann, just tell me about it."

"Ah… I don't know how to put it. I think I have changed my mind about my marriage to Henry but I don't know how to tell him."

"What!" Sophie asked. "That's unreasonable Ann. Look at where you two started and how far you've gone. This will break his heart and God knows you will mess up his life. Please reconsider."

Ann felt hurt and angry too. But her anger wasn't against Sophie. It was at herself. She must have known well that accepting to marry Henry was a serious commitment. He had believed her and proceeded with the wedding plans. With the wedding cards printed, Henry would stop at nothing to push through with the plans. What made her more miserable was the realisation that she was falling out of love with him. For once she saw him as an opportunist rather than a saviour. The reality of her marriage to him haunted her now and she wished she could evade it at all cost. Unable to control her emotions she broke into sobs and left for solace in her bedroom. Sophie stayed shocked and helpless as she watched her walk away.

As they sat sipping coffee after supper, Sophie uttered something that sparked off a topic she had been avoiding: The topic of marriage. She asked Henry about the progress of their wedding plans.

"Our wedding date is already set as indicated in the cards Sophie. You don't need to worry about that. Nothing can stop me now, you know." Henry said looking at her encouragingly. Ann had pretended to be impassive over the topic but she saw an opportunity to speak.

"There's no need for hurrying things like that. That date is too soon isn't it Sophie?" she said pretending to stifle a yawn. "I am very tired. You should excuse me. I have to go to bed early." Sophie remembered their conversation in the afternoon and stiffened. She should have kept off the topic for Ann's sake. She thought regretfully. Henry didn't comment on the fact that he had spent an exacting day working while she had done nothing. He had noticed her reluctance over the topic and was beginning to worry about what lay ahead of their initial plans.

"I think there's every need Ann. I can't wait any longer and, the sooner the better." Sophie realised the tension beginning to emerge and took off with a slight excuse.

"I think I should let you two discuss. I have a call to make before I go to bed. Goodnight!" she said standing to leave.

Hoist with her own frustration, Ann grew irritated. She found Henry the most maddening and frustrating of men. "Oh, don't be stuffy," she said as soon as Sophie exited and felt alarm begin to grow when he grabbed her hand and his grip tightened as his eyes narrowed. He didn't take kindly to being called stuffy, she couldn't doubt that.

"You called me something similar once," he grated rather than said. While his frowning alarm threatened to consume her, he stood up, pulled her from her seat and hauled her to his hard body. "You will live to regret this, I believe," he added and before she could stop him, his mouth had taken possession of hers. She struggled to free herself but to no avail. Henry wasn't finished with her and wasn't ready to heed any protest she made.

"Stop it!" she breathed when his mouth left hers. "I can't," he said trying to commence again but realising that she was determined to fight to the end, he released her showing disappointment. "What's happening Ann?"

"Nothing" Ann replied immediately but seeing the hurt in his eyes, she corrected her statement to; "I am sorry Henry. It's just that I am feeling tired and I have no mood for romance. Forgive me."

"It's okay. I feel tired too. Let's go to bed." He said realising that nothing he did would change her mood.

# CHAPTER EIGHTEEN

Ann found life without work boring and unbearable. She wished she could have something constructive to do to keep her busy. In Henry's house, she was not allowed to do any work; not even cooking. Everything was done by Diana; the housekeeper who appeared too efficient to require a helping hand. Whenever she tried to help, she would be reprimanded by Sophie who insisted it would mess up the status quo. She hated it because her background hadn't prepared her for the delicate lifestyle.

"I am free this afternoon Ann. why can't we go for window-shopping at Sarit. I am sure there are many pretty things you might wish to see." Sophie said over her plate of French fries.

"I would love to. This place bores me to death." Ann replied. "Then get ready. I want us to return before Henry comes back. He might think I am beginning to spoil you." Sophie said while standing to leave.

When they jumped into the bus heading back to the house, Ann felt relaxed and happy. Sophie was more generous than she had anticipated and had bought everything she showed interest in. Would she ever be in a position to do that for anyone if she accepted to be a housewife, she thought sadly. Sophie noticed her change of mood and asked. "What is it Ann. You were so lively at Sarit. I wish you would maintain that mood longer. I hate to see you looking miserable. What is disturbing you?"

"Nothing Sophie. I am fine. I only wish we could stay out longer. I always feel like a prisoner in that house."

"Oh Ann. Don't say that. We love you, and all we want is to make you happy."

"I wish I could see things the way you do Sophie. But I can't. We are in different worlds. You are free and working while I am tied up to your cousin and idle. I don't even see any hope of ever stepping in an office. My dreams are shattered Sophie. Can't you see?" She tried to control her voice that was almost getting hysterical.

"I am sorry Ann. But I think you are being too hard on yourself. Relax. Things will work themselves out. Everything is possible." Sophie consoled her

"Thanks Sophie. I hope so too". She said and they all broke into silence until they alighted from the bus.

As they approached the house, Ann was shocked to immobility when she saw Henry standing at the verandah. He must have come earlier than they had anticipated but why? She asked herself realising that Sophie would have serious explaining to convince Henry why they went out without informing him.

"Hello Henry!" Sophie said breezingly. "We have been out for a walk." She turned to Ann and then Henry and said; "you see I have brought your wife home safely."

Ann felt embarrassed but could not express it for Sophie's sake. She had to cover up her indifference to avoid further embarrassment.

"En-hello!" she threw the greeting his way as they approached him, her eyes fastened on the top button of the suit he wore.

"Hello yourself." His voice had a tender note to it which she knew was solely for his cousin's benefit; as was the arm that came about her and held her firmly as though he sensed she was about to pull away. Rigidly stiff in his hold, she felt his lips touch her cheek before he released her, then Sophie was informing him. "We were going to come and see you at work this afternoon, only Ann got shy. She was in quite a flirter about it actually."

"Thanks very much Sophie." Ann thought feeling Henry's eyes fixed on her and refusing to be cowed, she held her head up. He was looking at her, his eyes pinning her. She knew that he was wondering about the cause of her shyness, which he found difficult to understand. For him most ladies lost their shyness as soon as you got involved intimately. But Ann was different. What troubled his mind was the realisation that this behaviour could as well mean lack of interest, despite the efforts he had employed to buy her trust.

Maybe he was wrong himself. He thought sadly. It would as well symbolise her nature. May be she would never change. All these thoughts crossed his mind without realising it.

"I say, Henry," Sophie said into the silence noticing for the first time that he was in a suit after duty; a time when he normally wore slacks.

"You've set yourself up for something special today. What is the deal guy?"

"I have to go to town." He replied.

"Are you going for Ann's wedding ring?" She teased him before he could explain further.

"I don't need a ring this soon!" Ann stopped short when she felt herself fixed with a look that said, "Shut up." The rest of the words died in her throat and she hated him for being pushy.

"It's none of your business whatever I am going into town for. He said taking his eyes from Ann and softening his words to his cousin with a smile. Noticing the tension she had created with her outbursts, Sophie disappeared into the house.

As soon as Henry's car went down the drive, Sophie hurried out of the house. Ann in turn entered the house and sat in her favourite chair, silently fuming that if Henry had gone to buy her a ring, she wouldn't hesitate telling him what he could do with it. Sophie came back sooner than she had expected. To avoid questions from her, Ann excused herself and left for her bedroom. Ignoring her, Sophie went on to make a call and this gave Ann time to think over her crisis.

*Captive of Fate*

# CHAPTER NINETEEN

Ann lay in the double bed feeling sorry. Sophie came in uninvited as usual.

"Come on Ann. Stop languishing in that miserable bed. Put on your Jacket. I am treating you out."

"Out!" she responded with disappointment.

"Yaaap. I want us to have fun. Life here is boring to death. Since Mr. Bigman is out for the evening, why not grab the chance. I just rung Carey after Henry left and told him we would like to pick something at Pangani shopping centre. But you know what?" she explained quickly, "My aim is to get out and have fun with Carey. In fact, I told him it's you who wants to buy something but my intention is to trap him. That guy is gorgeous and I am prepared to do anything to get him into my hold although he appears conservative. Please!" she pleaded with Ann almost kneeling before her.

"But I don't need anything from town." Ann protested.

"I know you don't but it is a chance for me to be with Carey. You know how strict Henry is on me dear. All I need is some short moment with Carey. You can pretend that you want to buy something so that he can drop you at a joint where you can busy yourself till I come back to pick you. Please!" She persisted.

Before Ann could decide fully whether to comply, Sophie was already pushing her out of the house as she handed her, her favourite jacket.

In no time Ann found herself sitting in the back of Carey's Lagoon Sedate Salon car marvelling at the speed with which Sophie moved once an idea took root. She remembered how Sophie had worked out her relationship with Henry despite her reluctance.

Carey appeared to be the type of driver who liked to keep all his concentration on the job in hand. He hardly spoke except for his monosyllabic answers to Sophie's questions. The lights at Pangani shopping centre appeared and he turned his head to ask, "Where would you like me to drop you?"

"At the Mobil petrol station." Sophie replied for Ann which was just as well Ann's thought because she did not have a clue to the geography of the shopping centre. Sophie was a native.

When Carey stopped the car, she thought it was about time she played her part well and she was out of the car like a shot.

"I will have to dash" she said giving Carey her thanks. "The shops will close if I don't hurry." "I will meet you at the bus stage" Sophie said showing no signs of moving out. Ann raced away, only stopping when she was sure she would be lost to Carey's vision. She had no idea where the bus stage was and being a cold evening she hoped Sophie wouldn't keep her waiting too long. With so many people coming from the shops and offices, she had no difficult finding guidance to the bus stage, which was in front of a mosque.

Thinking of Sophie and her mad escapades as she went, Ann felt better than she had done all day. As she turned a corner at the Mosque exit, her good humour vanished. There was Henry's car parked. The number plates were too clear in the streetlights to doubt. With every intention of hiding in the nearest crowd, she was sure she would catch a sight of him. Glancing about her, she registered that the place where many people were standing by the road could be the bus stage and made for it. But just before she reached the real spot, she froze. Turning to the street on her left, she saw Henry and with him was a woman, obviously the one he had dressed executively to meet; and then all hell broke loose inside her. Shock, like a blow to her stomach lashed at her. "He's engaged to me". She wanted to shout with no thought in her mind that she had objected to it herself.

She watched, nausea gnawing at her; a sickness growing and rising as he and his mistress stopped while he said something. They looked intimate together, so much as though they belonged together that a blinding rage hit her that it should be so. She hated that woman and felt a need to physically attack her. But she restrained. She knew beyond doubt that Henry didn't belong to the sophisticated blonde. He belonged to her. But even with this conviction, the scene was still provoking.

She saw Henry place his hand beneath the woman's elbow and turned her in the direction of his car. They were coming her way. Wings on her feet, Ann fled round the corner. The thought of seeing those two heads close when they passed in the car left her feeling sick again. She took to her heels and raced into the alleyway. It was dark there, which is what she wanted most.

Leaning against the wall, she shook uncontrollably before gradually the shock of what had happened isolated itself from intuitive movement, impression and actions. She who placed such a high value on fidelity had seen Henry, who was pressing her for a hand in marriage with another woman. She had lost sight of the fact that she didn't even consider herself engaged to him. But still, she could not believe that the only reason for leaving his work early was to meet this mysterious woman. She wished she had a clue as to who the brat was. Seeing the two of them rocked her where she stood and brought to life a new screaming, tearing emotion: A hateful, all encompassing jealousy. She had been evidently angrily jealous that the man who pretended he couldn't live without her and pressed her for a wedding had left work that day so early so as to meet with another woman, more attractive than herself.

Ann was quite aware that she was being idiotic because in reality, she didn't have any real hold on Henry. But inside her she felt that he was being unfair. He was destroying her trust in him and blocking her vision as his wife. This knowledge was shattering. The most unfortunate thing was the realisation that she could not hate him completely. May be he was being fair to himself after she reluctantly, responded to his marriage proposal, she thought bitterly feeling confused over the whole issue.

It was fortunate Sophie had sweet-talked Carey into taking her for a cup of tea while Ann did her fictitious shopping; or else, she would have had half an hour to wait. It took Ann a long time before she felt she had sufficient control to move from her hide out to the bus stage.

Sophie sticking her head out of the car window and calling "Ready!" made her aware that she was still with Carey and not pedestrian as she had supposed.

"Carey says there won't be any bus back home for over the next one hour so he has offered to drive us back. Isn't that sweet of him?" Sophie quacked.

Carey was his usual silent-self on the return journey. "Did you get what you wanted?" Sophie asked from the front seat. Without waiting for an answer, she centred all her attention on the man besides her without noticing that Ann had not responded to her question.

In the silence that prevailed throughout their drive home, Ann wondered why she dropped Kombo for infidelity. Relating Henry's behaviour with Kombo's, she felt dizzy and wondered why she ever thought Henry was different. "Men will always be men," she thought bitterly resolving never to trust any.

As these things went through her mind, she began to realise why she had been affected by Kombo's betrayal so much. It wasn't because she loved him deeply. It was because he had shattered her faith in him by breaking that bond of trust she held so dearly. And now that Henry had repeated the same mistake, it hurt like hell. She tried to be logical but realised logic had very little influence over her emotions. It was true she hadn't considered her engagement to Henry serious but he did. Nevertheless, she couldn't marry him now. Not when on the very day he had assured Sophie that they were to be married, she had witnessed with her own eyes his inconsistency.

Dark destroying jealousy gnawed at her again when she pictured him with his lady-love but she was glad they had arrived home where she would have chance to sob down her bitterness. Thanking Carey for the lift, she jumped out of the car and left Sophie talking to him.

# CHAPTER TWENTY

U p in the bedroom, she stared at her reflection in the mirror. Her face was dull and her eyes shocked. She didn't feel like eating but she would have to put on a good face. Henry wouldn't be in for dinner, which was a blessing since she did not know how she was going to react to his presence again. But inside she still felt some love for him and this amazed her. Besides, circumstances seemed to push her into succumbing to the marriage proposal but the question still remained; how could she continue to trust him after he had betrayed her?

She selected the first dress at hand to change into as she prepared for dinner but as she did this, the same thought recurred in her mind and with it that searing pain. Was this how women felt when they discovered that their husbands had broken their marriage vows of fidelity? If so, she thought, then most women who opted to lead single lives were justified. And not just them, but those who chose to be unfaithful in return.

"I thought you might have worn the velvet dress you wore last night" Sophie interrupted her thoughts as she came into the room and surveyed the snugly fitting black dress Ann had on.

"Though come to think of it, you look stunning in that one too. I wish I was taller" Sophie complimented.

As they left the bedroom for the dining room, Ann wished Sophie wasn't going to be too inquisitive this evening. She wasn't in a mood for any conversation, no matter how friendly. But she shuddered when she went into the dinning room only to find Henry standing there looking relaxed and at much ease, wearing the same suit he had on in town.

Startled beyond her power, she made no attempt to go anywhere near him. Her mind went jealous over the time he had spent with his mistress. He had kissed her, hadn't he? She thought.

"What can I get you Ann?" Henry asked moving to stand by her side but she moved a step away when she thought his arm was going to come round her waist.

"Don't touch me!" she muttered in an angry undertone so that Sophie wouldn't hear. She couldn't bear that he should dare think he still had a right to put his filthy hands on her soon after coming from another woman.

"Not contagious, is it?" His voice sarcastic was equally low. Then as if noticing the moodiness of her expression for the first time; the way she looked ready to flinch if he so much laid a finger on her, he asked sharply, "What's wrong? What has upset you?"

"Nothing" she said carelessly. Then, she became aware that Sophie was looking at them. Forcing a smile on her lips, she said, "I won't have a drink tonight. Thank you Henry!" She knew he was teasing her about the drink because he was fully aware that she didn't drink beer.

Over dinner, Sophie let it out that they had been in town at Pangani shopping centre.

"I would have given you a lift if you had asked," Henry said, his eyes going speculatively to Ann as though he suspected that her going to Pangani had something to do with the way she was behaving.

Ann knew that she was behaving far from normally with him though she didn't care considering the circumstances. She hoped Sophie would put it down to shyness if she discovered that she avoided looking into Henry's eyes whenever he addressed her.

"Actually, Henry" Sophie told him candidly, "You weren't the driver I wanted."

"I see." He said catching on immediately. "When do you intend to move out?"

"Meaning you think I might corrupt your innocent wife if I continue staying around much longer?" Sophie replied.

Henry's expression was serious as he surveyed her but said nothing. Ann realised the tension beginning to rise and remembered that the excuse of a headache she had intended to use would come in very useful. She pondered over this thought as she saw Sophie drain her coffee cup and made to leave.

"Would you mind if Ann and I left you earlier for bed today? She looks unwell." Henry told Sophie.

Ann felt frustrated. Realising that her plans would not work now, she shot a disagreeable look at him, not wanting to get in to bed with him tonight. She had changed her mind over the headache excuse. She wanted to stay and watch a movie till Henry was deep asleep. But could he accept that? She wondered. It was perhaps too late. She regretted why she had let her dullness dominate her looks the whole evening. If she hadn't appeared that dull, at least Henry would have gone to the study room while she sneaked to bed alone. He would then find her asleep, either practically or hypocritically.

Not wishing to offend Henry any more, Sophie shrugged and said, "It's okay. Good night Ann." She then stood and left for her bedroom.

Ann hoped Henry would take her appearance seriously and let her sleep in peace but to her disappointment, she realised that he had no intention of waiting until they went to bed. The door barely clicked behind Sophie before he was saying, "Perhaps now that we haven't a third ear, you will tell me what upset you."

She was about to say, "nothing" as she had done before but she realised that Henry wouldn't let her get away with it. By implying that whatever had upset her was something she didn't want Sophie to hear, he knew fully well that whatever had upset her was something to do with the two of them only.

"I…"She began but didn't know how to continue. Telling him the truth that she had seen him in town with a woman and had been torn apart by jealousy would make him feel great and think she was desperately in love with him. This would give him the guts to misbehave further.

She looked cross at him and saw he was waiting with every semblance of patience. From the look of things, he had every intention of sitting there until midnight if need be or however long it took her to spit out whatever was troubling her. A new kind of anger invaded her, an anger that froze all heat, leaving her icily cold.

"I can't marry you," she said stonily, her chin firm and her look resolute. For her, it was for real. It had nothing to do with the fact that Henry had no reason to marry her as she did, she just couldn't marry the type of man she had discovered him to be.

Henry did not reply immediately to her blunt statement, but she didn't care. She didn't have feelings any more; just this terrible coldness that wouldn't leave. Her head high, she looked at him again, and the ice in her fractured marginally to see that he was not looking at her with the same look that demanded answers but a strange one. It was as if he was seeing her for the first time.

As he continued to look at her unmoved, she wondered if he was accepting what she had said and was planning to tell her to vacate his house. She couldn't bear it any longer. She was intending to leave with or without his permission. And then, he released a long drawn breath before his voice came forth as though he was disciplining it to stay even.

"May I know what reasons you have for breaking our engagement? He asked steadily and Ann marvelled at the steadiness of his question even when he knew fully well that by meeting his mistress at the first opportunity, he hadn't acted like an engaged man. She felt the fracture of ice within her turn into solid sheet once more.

"I don't know how you feel about things such as fidelity Henry. But for me, it means quite a lot." A cold stubbornness remained about her and she refused to look away as his eyes narrowed at her, on implication that he was a cheat. His voice matched hers in coldness when he said "Few things come higher to me than fidelity and trust, be it business or the subject we seem to be discussing. That's marriage." He sounded so sincere that she would have believed him had she not seen him in town with another woman.

She would have hit him when he grated at her: "Are you implying that I have acted perfidiously?"

"You know damn well, you have" she replied, her voice rising as she dared him to deny it.

"There's more than one way of breaking faith." He retorted, his tone hard. "Obviously you saw me in town with Mercy, a business associate but instead of trusting me, you straight away rushed to put your own conclusion on that meeting. I expect you to be more reasonable than that."

"Oh, very neat." She snapped angrily, "You sound just like Kombo whenever I caught him ready-handed. He could lie his way out of a paper bag to make me believe I was the one on the wrong to think such a thing of him"

"Your ex-boyfriend cheated on you and that's why you can't trust me." Henry said calmly when she thought he might leap over the table and throttle her for calling him a liar. Not that she cared, but it did puzzle her that instead of either verbally or physically attacking her, he looked at her as though wanting to know what made her what she is now.

"I should think you know." She replied cynically.

Henry didn't confirm whether he knew or not but his expression softened as he said, not urgently; "That has scared you, hasn't it? Left you in a state you can't trust an adult relationship between a mature man and woman."

She didn't want him to be gentle with her. It was getting through her defences just as Kombo had managed to get through. This thought was enough to have her anger rise again.

"Not at all" she denied woodenly but she knew it was plain truth. Her relationship with Kombo had cracked because she didn't trust him. Her temper fizzled out as these words shot from her leaving her to her horror, feeling as though she would break down and cry any moment.

"Let me go!" she said loudly when his arms came about her. But pushing him as she tried, he wouldn't let her go.

"Hush," he said softly, enfolding her and pressing her head against his chest. "Hush and listen to me Ann," he instructed, no hardness in him at all as he gently stroked her back.

"Let me go!" she repeated, her voice not loud anymore, but sounding nobly in her own ears. Even though she hated him, it was heaven to be in his arms. Oh, how could she be so weak.

She wondered as tears spilled from her eyes. She stopped struggling to get away from him knowing she couldn't bear him to see her tears. Perhaps she could secretly dry her eyes before he let her go but it also seemed impossible to stop the flow of her tears.

Henry continued to hold on her even when she was no longer struggling. Then, with his voice still gentle he said, "Had you asked me outright what I was doing meeting Mercy from her place of work, I would have told you."

Anticipating a whole chain of lies, Ann shuddered in his arms. "Please don't," she wanted to say, but the words wouldn't come.

"Was she expecting you to meet her?" she asked instead from her choked throat.

"I telephoned her this morning to see if she would be there. She works in the Planning Department and she is sometimes out inspecting property from where she goes straight home."

"So you arranged a date with her?" she asked in a muffled voice. The pain of the question like a knife thrust into her.

"If you like" he agreed. "Whatever I had to say to her, I wanted to say it as soon as possible yet I didn't want to tell her over the phone."

She stirred in his arms at the realisation that she may have overreacted. "Oh God, this is ridiculous. He had rushed to tell his girlfriend about their engagement before she could hear from someone else." She cringed. The sophisticated blonde must have laughed herself silly if he described the type of woman he was betraying her for." She thought sarcastically.

"How did she react to your information?" She asked hoping that her imaginations were right.

"Oh… I had expected her to react negatively. I told her that I wouldn't be seeing her again but she didn't react badly, she simply shrugged and said, "It's upon you." His hand moved gently to the side of her face to smooth away her tears.

"Then!" Ann persisted.

"She took her purse and stood to leave."

"You told her…" She began, her eyes shimmering with joy. She dived to bury her head in his chest again. There had been such sincerity in his face that she knew all he had told her were not lies.

Grateful that he had made it so easily in convincing her, he asked, "Do you believe me now?" "Yes I believe you. I am sorry…"

"Forget it." He brushed her apologies aside. "Well, I must understand what a sensitive person you are; bruised with every confrontation you encountered in your relationships especially with Kombo. You have a right to distrust me Ann."

Gently he tipped up her face and mopped at her damp eyes with his handkerchief. And then he said, "Trust me Ann. Trust me and marry me." Her head went down, but his hand beneath her chin forced it up again so that he could see into her eyes.

"I… trust you," she managed to tell him.

"And…" He prompted.

"And…" She begun, but hesitated and changed her response to a question. "Is Mercy in love with you?"

If it wasn't what he had been expecting to hear, then it didn't throw him off balance. Without hesitation he said, "No, we've been friends for a long time. But she was never in love with me."

Ann digested this, having to stamp down hard on giving her mind free range at the minute pause he had given before bringing out the word 'friend'. She tried to oust jealousy and tried to think calmly. He was a grown up man, for goodness' sake and a monk's behaviour wouldn't have suited him anyway.

"Were…" She too had to pause before she asked, 'were' she repeated again and changed to "are you in love with her?"

"No Ann. I am not in love with Mercy, and never was." He stopped to consider her but hardness lurking there when he added. "So if that clears up all your questions, are you going to answer the one I asked you?" He meant whether she was going to marry him. That she knew. "Yes", she replied.

"Good." He said his tone even, then he prevented her from saying anything more by changing the topic. "You are pretty emotionally used up. Why not go to bed and make an early night of it?" Without waiting for her response, he leaned down and kissed her good night.

Ann was on her way to the bedroom before she had time to think he hadn't given her a chance to respond but instead, he had promptly opened the door and pushed her through. He had said she was emotionally used up and he was right. She just wasn't thinking as she floated down the corridor to the bedroom. She barely saw Sophie coming from the other direction.

"You've been crying," Sophie accused her when she was near enough to see her face.

"Have I?" Ann replied and without saying more, opened the bedroom door. About to follow her into the room, Sophie halted; her anxiety for her friend diminishing. Whatever had upset her, Henry should have put it right.

"Good night, Sophie" Ann said. "Sleep well, Ann." Sophie said lightly turning away with a shrug. "Pleasant dreams," she added.

In bed, Ann couldn't sleep. She lay wide awake wondering how it was possible to love someone so much that they occupy every moment of your life and feel so angry; angry enough to hate when you suspected them of fishy deals. Finally, she fell asleep.

# CHAPTER TWENTY ONE

Ann lay in bed after a refreshing night's sleep reminding herself of the thoughts she had before sleep claimed her. By the time she woke up, Henry wasn't in the house. She couldn't tell whether he had left for some place or was just outside in the garden. Her bedside clock struck 9.00am and she felt it was time to jump out of bed and face the new day. After brushing her teeth and taking a bath, she went to the kitchen and found breakfast ready, prepared by Sophie. Instead of taking their breakfast in the dining room, the two friends decided to have it in the kitchen. Sophie was glad to see Ann in a bright mood compared to the gloomy one that had dominated the previous evening.

Ann was leaning on the sink, sipping her cup of tea when she caught a glimpse of Henry. Her heart leapt and started to race when she saw him go by the window. "He's coming in," she thought wondering if she looked all right. Was her hair style right? Should she have won a trouser suit rather than a sweater and jeans? But then, her heart dipped because Henry didn't come in. The main gate bell rung as he got in at the door forcing him to turn back and talk to the visitor.

After breakfast, the day went on smoothly with Ann and Sophie carrying out some cleaning chores in the house while Henry relaxed on the couch. As they sat in the dinning room having lunch, the telephone rung. Ann jumped up to pick it but Henry stopped her and went for it himself. When he returned, he informed her that he had to leave for abrupt business in town and couldn't tell how long he would be out.

When he left, Ann wouldn't help wondering if he could meet Mercy in town again. But the thought didn't linger to wound her with that awful jealousy she found so nauseating. She trusted him somehow. She knew if he did see her, then the meeting would be accidental. She realised that she was beginning to fall in love with Henry after resenting him all through.

As time continued to elapse without his return, she began to feel impatient. Her watch struck eleven o'clock but there was no point of putting out the light since she knew she was going to remain awake for hours. She hadn't seen him at dinner when she had confidently expected him and he hadn't had the decency to call and register that he would be late either. How could he be so loving at times and so careless at others? What kind of man was he? She asked herself struggling to convince herself that he wasn't with Mercy. The turning of the bedroom lock alerted her that she was about to have company. It wouldn't be Sophie, because she had the habit of hurling herself in like a whirling wind. Her heart leapt at the thought of his arrival and her hostility against him melted, her anger disappeared, shyness taking its place as she pulled the covers up to her chin, all too conscious of her flimsy night dress.

The door pushed inwards, and it was Henry. She swallowed several times while he half turned to close the door.

"All finished?" she inquired brightly watching as he came over to the bed. There were lines of tiredness around his eyes and she felt a mean short temper grow that she had ever been angry with him for his neglect.

"Just!" He sat down on the edge of the bed, his eyes full on her. She thought he was about to smile, then he observed the way she was hugging the cover to herself and the smile didn't come.

"I hoped you would still be awake," he told her. "I shall be away early and I won't be able to see you for sometime. I hate the thought of you spending cold nights alone in this bed but I have no otherwise. You will have to forgive me dear. It's business."

These words hurt her deep. She wished she would guess how long this separation was going to take. Could she really endure it or she should insist on joining him on the journey. But there was Sophie who would require her company, more than he did at this moment. She had to be considerate. It's this thought that forced her to change her decision and stay.

"I wanted to ask you to keep an eye on Sophie for me while I am gone." He interrupted her thoughts. Thank God for pride she thought. "Of course," she replied, keeping her eyes veiled.

"Normally I would hesitate to ask you to shoulder my responsibilities and Sophie does seem to have quietened down considerably since she became infatuated with Carey."

"Yes, I think she has," she said with an even politeness. "You are so good for her," Henry commented.

Ann allowed her lips to crack in a conventional smile but she felt her heart leaden as Henry pushed his hand inside his trousers' pocket and extracted something. Then, instead of showing her what it was, he bent to kiss her while his right hand sought for her left hand and fixed a ring on her middle finger.

She pulled away from his kiss to look at her finger. She gasped at sight of the gold ring resting snuggly at the base of her middle finger. How could it be? She wondered.

With a ring glittering on her middle finger, Ann was convinced that Henry was serious. He was ready to make her his wife. Every resisting thought began to give way to a receptive one. Strangely, as she lay calm on Henry's breast, she began to imagine of how their children would look like. Absorbed in this hallucination, she fell asleep.

When she woke up the next morning, Henry had left. Tears burnt in her eyes when she saw a note on her bedside stool. Instantly, she picked it and then turning to the bedside clock, it indicated 10.00am. Why did she have to oversleep on this day of all days? She regretted. She tried to wake up and read the note while sitting but she couldn't. She felt weak and dizzy. "What's wrong with me?" she wondered as she gathered strength to rise again but she couldn't. When she tried again she felt the same. Then suddenly she remembered that she had lost appetite the previous evening. The smell of food had nauseated her but she had ignored it thinking it had to do with her anxiety over Henry's whereabouts. She stretched and picked her small diary on the table and then after counting some days, her mind went blank. A scary thought had suddenly invaded it;

the thought of pregnancy. She didn't really know how pregnant women felt but she just presumed.

"You idiot," she reproached herself when she recovered from her shock. She felt even weaker from the horror of having messed up her life so carelessly. May-be Henry wasn't prepared for the responsibility yet and worse enough, he would think of it as an intentional trap. She opened the note and tried to read but she couldn't understand even a word. Tears flooded her eyes, and then, she broke down into sobs.

Sophie should have been listening at the door, because as soon as she calmed down, she burst in, in her usual manner.

"Ann...!" she began and then stopped dead. "Oh! Your poor swollen eyes" coming nearer to the bed she remarked, "Never mind love. He will soon be back."

To Sophie, Ann was crying because of Henry's departure, but that was not the case. Then catching sight of her ring, she blurted "Yoick! When old Henry falls, he falls with a bang, doesn't he?"

Sighing inwardly, Ann knew that things weren't well on her side. She wanted to remove the ring and explain everything to Sophie but she couldn't, till Henry returned. Her feelings of hurt were edged with a feeling of guilt that the whole mess was her fault. "Men don't take precautions. They don't care. It's the woman to be careful because she is always the victim," she thought bitterly. But it was too late for self-reproach. She had to be strong and think of how to handle the situation carefully.

As days elapsed, tired with the self-inflicted punishment of her thoughts, she came out of her mood of despondency to feel the aggression stirring.

Henry arrived on a Monday after being away for nearly three weeks. Sophie hadn't been a burden to her. They had had good time together visiting friends, going for movies and touring various parts of the city where she had never been before. This made her miss him less.

Early that Monday, she sneaked to a laboratory in town for a pregnancy test which came out positive. She prayed that Henry wouldn't reject the pregnancy. Shame and guilt made her feel terrible but she had to try and be calm. In the afternoon, she managed to convince Sophie to accompany her to a Christian crusade in town at Uhuru Park. The meeting ended later than they had anticipated. She felt guilty especially knowing very well that Henry had called announcing his arrival that evening. He would be hurt to find an empty house. She hoped that he would delay in town till late but her hopes were dashed when they reached home.

As they approached the gate, Sophie noticed Henry's car in the yard and pronounced that he had arrived.

"Henry's back!" she whooped. Then as though expecting Ann to be right behind with the same excitement to meet him, she wheeled off through the half open gate towards her cousin who was standing in the verandah of the main door. She hugged him before she turned to look at Ann.

"Aren't you excited?" Ann shook her head. She felt confused. All that she had planned to recite vanished.

"Poor Ann!" Sophie gave her a sympathetic grin. "You won't be as shy as this with Henry after your wedding."

Henry stood perplexed at Ann's behaviour but still held Sophie by her waist. His look at Ann wasn't that of anger but was that of encouraging her to come over and meet him. Ann still looked confused.

With Sophie's seldom remark about her wedding, her senses got alert and as if switched on by some unknown force, she hurried on towards them, wishing she could be again the girl she had been; the girl who seldom cried.

"After, your wedding!" she thought, and was fighting tears again. "There might be no wedding after all. Now that she was pregnant and didn't know how Henry was going to receive the news. God! Help me." She prayed as she approached them.

Ann felt unbearably hot at the thought of being held in Henry's arms. She felt her knees weaken as the distance reduced. Henry was still dressed in a well fitting light grey suit and her heart flipped over at just seeing him look so handsome.

Henry let Sophie off and made for her but this move scared her instead. Conscious of Sophie's presence, she wouldn't stand the embarrassment of being kissed before her. As if Sophie realised that her presence contributed to Ann's behaviour, she vanished into the house.

Henry realised Ann's troubled state and felt disturbed. Something could be wrong somewhere but couldn't she wait and explain later. This type of welcome was disappointing but he couldn't show his dismay openly. He had to act responsibly.

As he reached for her, instead of embracing her to be repulsed violently, he held her by her shoulders, looked straight in to her eyes and asked. "Have you had any problems Ann?"

"No". She said and groaned inwardly that she wasn't more sophisticated as she amended it to, "I mean, Yes but now that you've just arrived, my problems can wait".

"Coward," she reproached herself. Oh God what a chicken coward she was. It was no good saying she wouldn't have been so cowardly if she didn't love him as she did now. "Why not corner him, abort, cover it up and forget all about it. After all nobody knows." This imagination invaded her mind but she quickly dismissed it. It was evil and unforgivable to destroy life, innocent human life created by her on wayward passions and pleasure. It was the most selfish thing to imagine.

As if he understood her state of mind, he kissed her cheek and requested her to get into the house. It was getting cold outside. Relieved to be granted this chance, she made straight for the bedroom to drain the clouds of tears that were choking her eyes.

Ann heard the noise of pans in the kitchen and felt glad that Sophie was responsible enough to get to the kitchen alone. As soon as she got into the room, she kicked off her shoes, jumped on to the bed and let herself sob off her misery. She didn't even bother to switch on the lights.

The lighting in the room announced somebody's presence in the room. Possibly Henry and she had to control her sobs. As she strained to calm down, she heard him lock the door and knew it was the time to square out things. Sitting beside her on the bed where she lay, Henry turned her face to face him. She looked so miserable that he was moved to comfort her but he couldn't. Something had to be terribly wrong and he was becoming impatient. Wiping her tears he said gently, "You had better tell me what it is that's disturbing you." His tone was inviting.

"It can wait." Ann hedged. "Spit it out Ann," he shook her roughly.

"I can't marry you." The words left her mouth bluntly, rocketing out, fired by his rough attitude.

Henry stiffened and released her as though she had struck him with a knife. "Why the abrupt change Ann? Why do you hate me? Is it because you can't trust me?"

"No." She mumbled, lowering her head. She wished he hadn't started on that topic. "In that case, I think we are off to a flying start, don't you?"

"Yes…No." Did every woman in love have moments of difficulties with her own language? She wondered, not sure of what she wanted to say anymore.

Henry smiled as though reading her thought. Then, ignoring completely that she had just stated that she couldn't marry him, he said gently, "We could have a good marriage Ann". I know you have been scared by your nervousness."

Ann tried to keep her face deadpan while Henry went on, "But you and I hold the same views on fidelity. I shall never let you down. Trust me" he pleaded.

"Oh, I do trust you", She said, "But…"

"But you are not sure of this step we are about to take?" He smiled again, encouragingly. "Have no fears my dear." He sounded convinced but he didn't know what she had to tell him yet. She gathered all her courage to tell him the truth and was about to but Henry interrupted.

"Perhaps it would help you to realise how important our marriage is to me. If I tell you..." he stopped as though making an unaccustomed search for the right words. Ann felt as though she was on the edge of a precipice. Was he going to tell her that he loved her little? Oh God, could he? Did he? He looked so serious, she thought, her heart beating so wildly that she felt it would jump out of her chest. She could be insanely wrong, the thought dashed and just in case she was, she tilted her chin ready for the blow, keeping her face impassive. Henry studied the aloofness of her expression for a moment, and then went on slowly.

"I have a vast wealth which preludes me from being a lifelong bachelor. I am duty bound to marry sometime if only to ensure that my property is handed down to somebody."

"Oh!" Ann gasped. Being dumped in a bath of cold water was nothing compared to the terrible dashing of her ridiculous hope that encompassed her at these words. What an idiot she was? But pride kept her from seeing how let down she felt as she sought around in the boggle of her mind for some way to reply.

"You mean the sole purpose of your marriage to me is for an heir? Who do you think I am? Is it that the best you see in me is a good reproductive machine?"

"That's right," he nodded calmly ignoring the last phrase of the statement". "I should very much like you to be my wife Ann."

"Oh! What do you understand by the concept wife? Some property to acquire and use for selfish ends?" Her heart picked up its wild beat again. She could marry him of course, now that she was already expecting but his reason for marrying wasn't convincing. It was for procreation, not love.

"Why me particularly?" her inside started churning.

"You are beautiful, intelligent and more so reasonable."

"That's cruel Henry. Marriage means more than that or rather I expected more than what you are offering." She paused, seeking for the right words before proceeding. "By the way, if it's the heir you want, you have him already. I am pregnant, and I wouldn't mind mothering it for you and let you bring it up while I go my own way. I may at least find somebody who will love my soul and not just my body as you do."

Henry stiffened at the revelation. He just hadn't expected it so soon. But there was no need crying over spilled milk. This reaction angered her even more. She had expected him to jump and hug her. After all, he had made it clear that the purpose of their marriage was an heir. Then she remembered his sophisticated blonde whom he had said he had no interest in and commented. "I thought you dropped Mercy because she refused to give you an heir. Why then do you look perplexed at the good news?"

"Don't misjudge me Ann. My reaction has nothing to do with that. I told you that Mercy was just a friend and I don't see why she should feature constantly in our conversation any more." He sounded irritated but he had to control the emotion. As if speaking with a lot of difficulty, he said, "Ann, I love you very much. My problem is that, it came so soon. You see, my wedding plans are now in a mess. No pastor will agree to join us in his church in your state. But anyway, we may have to go to the Attorney General's Chambers. However, let's suspend that topic for now." He released a heavy sigh before saying, "I think I am washed up. I need a shower badly. And then, we can go for supper. I am very hungry."

As she waited for him while he bathed, Ann hated to believe that she was binding herself to this man for an heir rather than true love. She felt so miserable because she realised that her dreams were shattering again. Her future remained blank despite the achievements she had made. Remembering her first class B.A Degree lying in her suitcase, she wondered why she had worked so hard while her friends relaxed. She had to do something about her future. May-be she would write to the university seeking a scholarship for further studies, she thought deeply. For her, marriage was a total failure. It was no solution to her life's problems. In fact it seemed to mark an end to her career dreams; the beginning of worse problems. For a short while, she forgot about Henry and the marriage crisis.

Through out dinner, she was so quiet that Sophie began to sense something wrong. But she couldn't ask then. She could wait until Henry was away, and then she could make a move to find out the truth.

# CHAPTER TWENTY TWO

Ann woke up at 10 o'clock feeling tired and bored. She was barely five months in her marriage to Henry yet her marriage seemed to be disintegrating already. Business meetings had increased and she conversed with Henry more over the phone than in person. She felt lonely and frustrated with nobody close to share her grief with. Sophie had left Henry's house soon after their marriage. The only people she could now turn to were Grace and Faith, her old friends at the university but she couldn't dare reveal her frustrations to them because they had advised her against the marriage. Faith and Grace still held on to their Christian convictions and continued to persuade her to return to her faith because God was ready to forgive her rebellion. Faith always assured her of support incase she underwent any crisis or even changed her mind about her marriage. At that time she was working with an international airline and felt confident to support Ann if need arose. Grace ran a boutique in town. They both claimed to have no hurry for marriage because God would provide the right men for them at the right time. As her crisis continued to deepen, Ann began to realise the truth in their advice and to a certain extent, she was willing to reveal her real situation to them. She had to, because if she didn't, she would break down.

It was a Saturday morning. Ann hadn't seen Henry for three days. Not that he had failed to call. He had always called and informed her of his coming but later on cancelled his promise with an apology or an excuse of more business coming up and holding him up. She felt miserable. She had to find something to keep her busy to ensure that she had forgotten about him for sometime. She had requested him to find her a job but he had dismissed it as ridiculous. At around two o'clock, she decided to get out of Henry's haunting house and go to town for a change. Since she had nothing important to do in town, she decided to go to Uhuru Park and find out if there was anything interesting to keep her mind occupied and then move on to see Grace at her boutique.

On her way to town, her mind wandered back to Henry. Was he really busy doing business or was he playing games? And, even if he was on business, where was he finding clothes to change for three days if he wasn't keeping a mistress somewhere! Still absorbed in these thoughts, the bus stopped just near the park where she had intended to go and when she realised that she had reached her destination, she rose to join the alighting passengers.

As she strolled towards the swimming pool, she noticed a crowd of rowdy people, both young and old including women with children, carrying placards and posters. The scene attracted her attention and she had to stop and find out what the situation was before making further advance.

"They should be demonstrating against the tribal clashes," she thought when she remembered the political situation at that time.

The tribal clash crisis had rocked the country in almost in all provinces threatening the stability of the nation while the rate of inflation had sky rocketed. Unfortunately, political opportunists hijacked the opportunity to blame it all on the government and taking advantage of the hungry, bitter and frustrated masses, riots and acts of lawlessness were fuelled to make the government ungovernable. As she pondered over this, she remembered her days in Campus when rioting was fun and felt inspired to join the mob. At least this would give her something to occupy her mind.

"BAN THE CLASHES OR RESIGN", the banner attached to a stout lady's chest announced quite clearly. "PEACE EVERYWHERE," declared a large board held aloft by a bearded young man. "OLE MANGUT AND PARLIAMENT WORRIORS SHOULD RESIGN" stated a ragged piece of cardboard clutched gamely by a harassed Kikuyu woman, also accompanied by two untidy looking children by her side.

Along the Uhuru highway, heading into the park was a group of young men and women possibly students from Nairobi University marching towards the Park. As they entered in the Park, there was a milling crowd around the freedom square among whom was Ann. She was squashed between an earnest looking group of young girls with long untidy hair and grubby looking outfits and a bespectacled gentleman who kept muttering to himself. Ann looked attractive with her long hair concealed beneath a chiffon scarf. She wore a cream channel suit, which looked out of place in the company where she was. Glancing around, she felt funny standing there as part of the crowd without Henry. In their honeymoon days, she seldom did anything or went anywhere without him, but things had drastically changed. Long business trips and late meetings had become the order of the day. He seemed to be getting completely involved in his work, almost to the exclusion of everyone else. She sighed.

It was indeed by chance that she was at this meeting. Sitting alone in the house had become unbearable. She had to occupy herself somehow and for this day, this would do. The bespectacled man standing beside her suddenly looked at his watch. "It's three o'clock" he announced excitedly. There was a sudden surge forward of the crowd, a general shouting and yelling. Small groups of people began to disintegrate from the masses and rush towards the road where they promptly sat down in front of the traffic.

Ann was carried forward with a rush and found herself near the edge of the road. There were policemen pushing, dragging and lifting the squatters from the road after several blows using their 'rungus'. As soon as one person was removed, another one immediately took his place. The mob seemed delighted with the game. They chanted various slogans, cheered and booed at the police while some stoned them. The blue police cars gradually began to increase and riot police lories could be spotted parking at a distance. But undaunted, more squatters appeared.

Ann felt marvellous. "Stop the clashes" she shouted. "Expel the warriors from parliament." She was protesting about an issue of national value and felt involved in a meeting of national interest. She was in a minor way helping to protect the future of her nation.

"Stop the clashes." Joined in the people near her. "Come on, darling," a dark young man grabbed her by the arm and together they rushed on to the road where they sat in the way of an on-coming police car. "Bustards." The driver growled. The crowd began to stone the car. The driver, who was also a policeman tried to reverse in vain. Sensing loss of control the riot police jumped out of their Lories and descended on the unarmed crowd with their 'rungus'.

Ann had a feeling of complete exhilaration and then a dark faced constable was grabbing her under the arms and pulling her to the side of the road where a police car was parked. She started to struggle and another policeman joined them and took hold of her legs. There was a moment of immodesty as she felt her skirt hike up above her knees and then she was unceremoniously dumped on the pavement when the crowd overpowered the police. Helping hands got her to her feet only to discover she had lost her shoes and cut her arm. Her scarf had vanished and her hair fell loose round her face.

"You look a right mess; don't you?" It was the same young man who had dragged her on to the road. "Want to give it another try?"

A girl grabbed him by the arm, "Oh, come on Paul, let us get out of here before we land in prison. The riot police have arrived. I don't want us to be clubbed."

Paul laughed and ignored her. "Look" he said to Ann. "You better come with us. I have got a friend who lives near here. We can or may get you some shoes."

"Well…" Ann started, feeling confused.

"Let us not hang about Paul," the girl said crossly.

"Alright," Ann decided and the three started to push their way through the crowd as the tear gas canisters began to explode. Paul took hold of her arm and guided her through the mass who were running in all directions. His girlfriend miserably trailed behind him.

"My name is Paul Kithinji, What's yours?" Ann glanced at him. He was tall. She guessed he could be about twenty-two. He looked uncomfortably attractive.

"I am Ann Odibo. Mrs", she replied. Paul looked disappointed but she didn't give him time to respond or add a word. Looking around to see where they were, she saw a number 56 bus stop for people to board and realising that it was going towards her home's direction, she shook her hand off the young man's grasp and jumped in, leaving them staring unbelievingly.

As she stood in the bus, she drifted into thought. "Henry is a good husband, a wonderful lover", She thought. But when did he make love to her these days? May be once a fortnight and then a quick and short affair out of which she derived no particular pleasure. Afterwards, he would turn over and go to sleep while she lay awake thinking of how it used to be. Sometimes he came home drunk and quarrelled without cause. It was horrible, she thought.

When she looked through the window she realised that the bus was approaching her bus stop. She hadn't paid her fare and was not sure if she had any money on her after the chaos in town. She hadn't even thought about it when she jumped into the bus. Instinctively, she slid her hand into her bra and fished out a twenty-shilling note. Thanks to God it was there. She couldn't even remember putting it there. After paying her fare and getting her balance, she moved to the door and waited for the bus to stop. When it did stop, she jumped off and began to walk home slowly feeling weak and tired.

The house was empty and haunting. Their live-in maid Diana was out for the weekend and it was depressing to be alone. Ann felt pain in her cut hand, but went to switch on the television before attending to it. She had no interest in watching the television but it was nice to have some human voice around her. Bored by the programme on the screen she left it on and went to the bathroom where she cleaned her cut and bandaged it.

After bathing and changing into another dress, she telephoned Faith and narrated to her the story about the riots in town. It was a joyful moment. She almost forgot about her miseries as they laughed and chatted over the phone.

"That was the most terrible thing you could afford Ann. How do you think Henry will react?" Faith asked.

"I don't care." Ann replied.

"You have to dear. Just pray that you don't provide an attractive cover-photo for the newspapers tomorrow. I am sure Henry would be mad."

"I wish it happens. It would be fun for me." Ann replied. Their conversation went on for some time before Faith excused herself and hung up after wishing her a goodnight.

"What now?" Feeling slightly hungry, she went to the kitchen but did not feel like cooking. She hated cooking for herself. After thinking for a while, she settled for a sandwich and a cup of coffee. Feeling too tired to hang on waiting for someone who might never turn up; she switched off the television and went to bed.

In bed, she could not sleep. Her mind was too turbulent to rest. "Bed, Henry," the two thoughts connected in her mind and an idea was formed. Jumping out of bed, she rushed to her closet and hunted around until she found what she was looking for; a slinky black velvet dress she had been bought soon after marrying Henry but never got around to wearing it. It had always seemed too frivolous but not now. She held it up against her and then rushed to iron it. "Well, this is what they say in all the women's magazines," She thought smiling. "Shock your husband into realising how utterly sexy and devastating you really are."

After ironing the dress, she changed into it and began to style her hair until it looked luxurious and inviting. Feeling satisfied as she stood before the full-length mirror, she was happy her tummy wasn't showing much. But her face looked pale and she had to do something about it. She started to cream it and powder it. After doing all this, she went back to the sitting room, switched on the television and forced herself to watch as she waited for Henry. Immediately, the phone rung. Knowing it was Henry, she reluctantly went to pick it. "Hello," she said softly.

"Hello darling," Henry responded. "How is everything there? Hope you are doing fine. For sure I am very sorry for being out too long. I know you should be missing me badly but just bear with me. The work is too much here in the office with countless business meetings." He paused briefly as though expecting her to respond but she remained silent. She was too angry to react. The best thing was to let him finish saying whatever he intended to say.

He must have realised that she was not going to respond so he proceeded. "Eh… I just called to inform you that I have a meeting scheduled from 9.00p.m to midnight. I may come in late. Therefore, have your dinner. Please don't wait for me." He hung up.

Ann wanted to scream at him and tell him that she was fed up with his behaviour but her voice couldn't come out. She banged the phone, locked the door and switched off the television. Feeling frustrated, she went to bed with tears burning her eyes. She didn't even bother to change into her nightdress. Feeling disappointed, she jumped into bed and broke into sobs. She cried until sleep caught up with her.

*Captive of Fate*

# CHAPTER TWENTY THREE

It was 4 o'clock when Henry and Mercy returned to her apartment. She lived in a flat at Garden Estate, all very new and modern. She occupied the top apartment, where had the advantage of no yard to maintain. Henry had often wondered how she afforded it. All her furniture was new and obviously expensive. She had an enormous wardrobe of clothes. Yet she was only an actress and a model, and from what he knew of both professions, unless one was extremely successful, you didn't earn much money. Certainly, not enough to keep her in the life style she obviously lived. Eventually he began to think that she might have a rich background but this didn't tie in with the bits and pieces of information he had of her background. According to the information he had, she had left home at the age of fifteen and arrived in Nairobi five years ago, all set to be a movie star. Now, she was twenty, very beautiful and sparkled like diamond, but was no successful movie star. He had known her for a long time. She was always available. There didn't appear to be any other man in the picture. She accepted the fact that he was now married and didn't nag him about it as a lot of women would. She never even mentioned money to him. He had seen her feature in some commercial advertisements for perfumes and local programmes like Tausi and Mawindo but apart from that, she hadn't worked at all. He decided that he would find out more about her. May-be she needed money but was too proud to mention it. He thought carefully. He had to find out.

When they entered Mercy's apartment, she rushed about making a great show of fixing the bed and tidying up. She was most undomesticated. She went to the kitchen and made a disgusted "ugh" when she came across the dirty dishes in the sink. Henry followed her in.

"I will buy you a dish-washer." He said slipping his arms around her waist. She turned laughing. "You are joking of course. A dishwasher! What a terrible present. I will have something more romantic than that. Thanks".

"What do you want? We will go shopping tomorrow," he teased her.

"I want, let me see now. I want a pair of jeans, two jackets, lots of diamonds and a villa." She started to laugh. "Can you afford me?"

"I am serious. I will settle for a Jeans jacket and a Jeans pair of trousers first. Go and order tomorrow"

She stared at him and licked her lips. "I would adore that. But if you want me to have them, surprise me. None of this ordering jazz. I like surprises."

He grinned. "A surprise it will be." He wondered if now was the time to bring up her financial issue but decided against it. Maybe later when they were in bed.

"When do you wish to return to Cinderella tonight?" she asked suddenly.

"I should leave at about eight thirty. He stroked her hair. "But I can always extend the time, depending on what the offer is."

Sometime later when Henry looked at his watch, he was surprised to find it was past nine o'clock. Mercy lay asleep beside him. Her hair in disarray and her make up smudged and faded. She looked very young. Her clothes were scattered around the bedroom, leaving a trail from the kitchen. When she sensed him looking at her, she opened her eyes, yawned, stretched and made contented noises.

"You are a cat." He said, "Sometimes an innocent little kitten and sometimes the wildest, dirtiest alley cat around."

"I like that. I can see myself telling it to someone else in the years to come. There was this guy, and he said to me, "you are like a cat, sometimes." He put his hand over her mouth. "Don't say that. There will be no other guy. It's only me. I love you and I want to marry you." He surprised himself with the words, but there they were spoken, aloud for all to hear.

"You know, it's amazing," she said, "how very simple it is for married men to propose. I guess it's an easy thing for them to say because actually, they are all safe and secure and they know they can lay out this tasty bit of bait without a hope in hell of getting trapped themselves."

"Marry me, my darling, only don't let my wife find out!" He was furious. So all right, he hadn't meant it. Correction, he meant it, but as she had thought, he was secure in the knowledge that it was not possible. However, the fact that she realised this infuriated him. Why did women always seem to have so much insight into the things men said?"

"I could get a divorce," he offered.

"Are you going to? You are barely five months in your marriage," she replied coolly.

"I don't know!" He pulled her to him. "It's not just me and Ann. There's a child she's expecting. But I do love you and one day, when she has given birth, everything will be okay. In the meantime, I can look after you. I don't want you to work. I will give you money."

She stared up at him with her large slaughter eyes. "I am glad you have it all figured out." She caressed his face. "There's only one little problem. I don't want to marry you. Not even if you were single. I want to be free. No ties, no strings. I don't want marriage. It means nothing to me. So, don't offer it like it is a golden hoop because I am not going to jump. So, I love you now, today. But tomorrow who knows? That's me. I don't pretend to be someone I am not. So, why not do the same?"

For Henry, it was devastating. When he was with Mercy, it always, was part of him. Each time, it was more, emotionally and physically.

"You'd better get up. It's past the watching hour and your wife will be waiting.

"Don't be a bitch. Anyway, I think I'll stay."

"Oh! That's great. Congratulations" she teased him.

Together, they phoned Ann. Mercy pretended to be the operator at the exchange so that the call would appear as if it came from the office. They then got up and she busied herself in the kitchen making sandwiches while Henry prowled around the flat thinking of how he could bring up the subject of finances again. She had annoyed him with the stupid speech about not wanting to marry him. He didn't really want to leave Ann. In his own way, he loved her. For him, she was the perfect wife figure. A lovely hostess and would make a perfect mother. He thought and smiled. No, he certainly didn't want to leave her. He felt no particular guilt about being unfaithful to her. Although if she was to him... "But no." That was unthinkable. The very idea of Ann being unfaithful was ridiculous.

He didn't spend the night at Mercy's. They disagreed when he demanded to know who was maintaining her in the expensive flat. He decided to spend the night at Villa Hotel because it was a bit late. As he drove to the hotel, he was puzzled as to why Mercy was so secretive about the source of her income. It only meant that there was something he wouldn't like to hear.

After going through the hot and cold steam bath at the Villa, he was quite happy to settle down in his small white cubical where he promptly fell asleep. He would sort out things the next day.

After a while, Ann stopped crying. Where was that going to get her? She went into the bathroom and washed her face. She didn't know what to do. She knew she couldn't take the prospect of sitting around waiting for Henry to arrive home fresh from the arms of some tramp.

Henry left the Villa cubicle at eight in the morning feeling refreshed and invigorated. He contemplated calling Mercy but then decided to wait and see if she would call him. He went to the Mangoose Hotel, parked his car, bought a newspaper and made his way into the hotel for breakfast.

He ordered bacon, eggs, toast and coffee and sat back to scan the papers. His eyes were immediately caught by a half page coloured picture on the front of the Sunday Nation Newspaper. It was captioned, "MORE RIOTS AT UHURU PARK," The picture was of an angry mob of people surrounding two policemen who were in the process of carrying a woman away from the road. The woman's skirt was high above her knees, so high that you could see her panties. Her hair was a mess and one shoe was about to fall from her struggling foot. It was an effective picture. The waitress arrived with his breakfast order. She was plump. She peered over his shoulder at the paper.

"Eh, what does she think she looks like! It's about time all this rubbish was stopped. A lot of show offs. That's what they are. They should lock the lot of them up." She walked away.

Henry stared at the photo horrified. The woman was unmistakably Ann. He shook his head in disbelief. "What was she doing? What was she thinking of?" he wondered aloud. He gulped his coffee scalded his tongue, swore, found himself unable to eat, and called for the bill.

The waitress padded back slowly. "What's the matter dear? Is everything alright?" He thrust money at her.

"Everything is fine". He said as he stormed out. He drove away, his face grim. He envisaged what he would say to Ann. The whole thing was so utterly ridiculous. His pregnant wife at the protest meeting! It was ludicrous. She knew nothing about politics and clashes. The kitchen and social activities were her province. "Stop clashes, indeed!" who did she think she was? Mercy was forgotten. He put his foot hard down on the accelerator and raced home.

Diana ran to open the door when she heard him hoot. She then ran to the kitchen to prepare breakfast for him. When he came in she reported, "Madam. She sleeps late. I don't want disturb her. You like tea?"

"No", he grunted, already halfway to the bedroom.

Ann was asleep, curled up and buried beneath the covers. He drew open the curtains, throwing glaring daylight into the room. She didn't appear to show any signs of waking. He went over and shook her roughly, thrashing a copy of the Sunday Nation in front of her face as she sleepily opened her eyes.

Expecting courtesy from Henry was like expecting a pig to fly. "What's all this about?" he demanded angrily, his aggressively beaky nose almost increasing in depth. It was his nose that stopped the handsome man from becoming beautiful.

"Oh God! What is it?" Ann sat up quickly. Henry stood there glowering at her as he continued talking.

"What is this? Some secret ambition to make yourself look a complete fool?" He brandished the paper at her again.

She took it from him. "What an awful photo!" she exclaimed. "I didn't know they were taking snaps." She responded calmly.

"Is that all you have to say?" He mimicked her. "I didn't know they were taking snaps!" He snatched the paper away and in a loud and angry voice said, "What were you doing there anyway? What were you thinking of?"

"I had nothing to do. I just found myself there. I wish you kept me a bit busier than what I am now. But I am sorry about the whole mess. I didn't mean to anger you."

"I am not angry," he screamed.

"Do you think I would like to see photos of my wife with her skirt above her waist, accompanied by a load of lay-abouts!"

Ann jumped out of bed. "I am not going to sit here while you yell at me. I am no better than them. Perhaps if you spent a weekend at home for a change, this might not have happened. But in as much as you continue staying out for days, you should expect worse ones."

Just then, the phone rung. Henry swooped down on it and barked into the receiver. "Yes!" He then launched into a long conversation with someone from the office. She sat on the bed listening to the conversation. When he finished talking, he seemed to have calmed down.

"Do you want some breakfast?"

"No," I have to make some calls. He left the room and shut the door behind him.

# CHAPTER TWENTY FOUR

At the seventh month of her pregnancy Ann's health began to show signs of deterioration. Diana suggested that it was because of stress. "You have been straining yourself very much over your husband. Men are like that. Bother not child, with time, he can change. The best way to deal with men is to ignore what they do and pretend you are not seeing."

"Thanks for your concern Diana" she said. "But I can't pretend I am not seeing what Henry is doing. It is humiliating. I wish Sophie was here, may-be she could help me forget about him for a while. But he kicked her out because he thought she would spoil me. Diana I feel so lonely and miserable. I need something to occupy my mind if I am to erase Henry's haunting image. But there's nothing I can do. He can't even let me get a job or do some business. I..." She broke into sobs.

"Please child, don't strain yourself over this. Be strong or else you will die and leave him behind. He won't bother. He can marry. Therefore, take courage. God will find a way out for you." With these remarks, she excused herself and left.

"God will find a way out for you. That's a familiar phrase". Ann thought when Diana had exited. Her mother had always advised her to be strong because God would find a way out for her. Why hadn't she thought about her mother for a long time? She hadn't been home since she graduated from the University. That was about seven months ago. What were her parents thinking about her? She felt so guilty that she had to get out of the seat and walk to the garden to ease her mind. In the garden, the flowers looked wonderful and she envied them. But then she remembered how soon that blossom would fade and dry off when they matured. This thought drifted her back to her crisis. Feeling weak, she moved on and leaned against the wall beside the garden under the shade of a guava tree.

Yes, she had thought of committing suicide one time. But what could that benefit her. She remembered the high hopes she had had while in Campus and shuddered inside. What about her parent's expectations? Her death would be a disappointment and misery to her family: she had to be strong and do something about her life.

"I have to convince Henry and get to work as soon as I deliver," she resolved. The thoughts of quitting her marriage or committing suicide vanished for a while. "I have to try and win his love back even if it goes against my conscience," she began to feel excited.

With a refreshed mind, she walked back to the house to take a bath and dress up. She had to make herself attractive and surprise Henry that evening if he would at all remember to come home. It was a Sunday afternoon and possibly by 4 o'clock, he could be home.

The phone rang just as she entered the room. Without hesitation, she picked it.

"Hello! Odibo's house can I help you?" she asked when she realised that it was a woman's voice.

"Can I speak to Henry please!" "He's not in. Who's calling please!" She waited for a reply but nothing came. "May I know who's calling please." Instead of responding, the caller hung up and replaced the receiver on her end.

Feeling disgusted, she banged the receiver and went to the bathroom.

She was just applying her make up when Henry came in. It was a surprise and she couldn't hide her perplexity.

"You look wonderful in that dress. Where are you going to?"

"Mm, nowhere."

"That's great. I think I should take you out for dinner."

"Take me out?" the word came out without her intention and she hated herself for it. It was a unique evening. She didn't want to spoil it. She quickly corrected her response when she realised that he wasn't happy with her response. "Oh, I mean, that would be great.

Let's go for coffee. I am sure Diana has prepared it by now."

"That's okay with me." Henry replied. She ran to the kitchen to see Diana while Henry remained behind to change from his suit. A few minutes later, they were in the sitting room chatting and Ann felt it was a good opportunity to bring up her topic.

"Henry," she said suddenly, "I would like to go to work after I deliver this baby."

He couldn't have been more astonished if she had said she would like to jump off the top floor of a tall building. "You would what?"

"I have to have something to do. Something interesting. You are all wound up in the agency. I am all alone here and I find idleness terrible. It makes me dull and bored. I'd like to be more active."

He recovered quickly. "Well, fine Ann. Any idea of what you want to do?"

"Unfortunately, no. But I can do anything especially business.

"Business! No. I would hate to stay with another businessman in one house. Ann! I have enough money to keep you going through-out your life. Why bother yourself? Business is not as simple as you think. There are risks and I don't see the reason why we should risk our money starting another business when we've already established one."

"That one is yours. I want mine."

"But Ann, my property is yours too. You ought to be proud of it. Many women would wish to be in your shoes. Stop being big-headed and stubborn for nothing."

"Sure, poor Henry" she said. "You really should have married a helpless nitwit. Not a mule, like me." She came and sat in his lap. "Never mind darling. I know I am a little crazy, but I love you. Sorry for hurting your ego." She rose and moved away.

"Damn it! What made me say such an idiotic thing?" Henry fumed. She was being herself. "Why do I hate it when she's strong and self willed and independent? This is Ann. No different than ever," he smiled apologetically.

"That was a half-ass thing to say, Ann, forgive me." He came to where she was standing and tried to embrace her. "I love your idea but you've to consider my position!"

Ann shrugged him off, "It was a dumb idea, that one. Forget it Henry. I think I will find my way out. One thing I know is that I have to find something to do to keep me busy and make me financially independent to assist my family back at home. I hate being a parasite. I know you will hate it if I succeed, won't you? You would like me to be a damned doormat; the little timid wife at home, waiting with bated breath for the master's return, incapable of having any thoughts or ambitions of her own. Well this is 2007 and I suppose there are women like that; the ones who like being useless and brainless and pathetic, but you will have to look elsewhere for them. No", she added sarcastically, "Not that you haven't already, I am sure. One just called some minutes ago." She took off before he could respond.

"Just as well," Henry thought. What good was a terrible fight about something he couldn't really explain? "What has happened to us Ann? What's pulled us so far apart? Why are we drifting apart? Is it because we were never right for each other from the beginning? A bit late for that kind of speculation," he thought ruefully. Almost for the first time he realised Ann must be as troubled as he was. "I have hurt her badly with my refusal to comply with her request to work. But why should she? I have enough to give her all the comfort she needs. Even for her family. I will have to make her understand and see the sense in my point." He resolved.

# CHAPTER TWENTY FIVE

That woman called again today." Diana stopped short outside the living room door sensing from Ann's voice that this was not the time to enter. Guilty about eaves-dropping, but mystified and intrigued, she stayed quiet, waiting to hear the master's reply. Ann sounded contemptuous.

"For God's sake, don't pretend Henry. Not at this stage. You have made no secret of this one. Isn't it a little ridiculous to act as though you don't know whom I mean?" Her voice rose just a shade. "Your current mistress telephoned."

"I see. Sorry, my dear. I will make sure that it doesn't happen again. She knows better than to call here."

Ann laughed. It was not a pretty laugh. "You're incredible!" the laughter turned to accusation. "It's the same with every one of these poor, stupid women. They actually believe you want to marry them. Dear Lord, I almost feel sorry for them, taken in by your lies. How convincing you must be, playing the unhappy misunderstood husband and knowing all the way that you have no intention of changing the way you live."

Henry seemed perfectly calm. "Why should I change it Ann? My life is exactly the way I like it. I have a delightful wife and a gracious home. These others are totally a separate part of my life. They have nothing to do with you. Nothing to do with the love I feel for you. I love you dearly, you know. I wouldn't exchange you for anything in the world. I can't help it if some silly woman misinterprets my intentions. I am only sorry she troubled you."

Even from a distance, Diana heard Ann sign. "Why do you do it Henry? Why must there always be another woman?" She didn't wait for an answer. "And why do you think I should accept it? I would be ashamed if my friends and family knew what you do; More ashamed of myself than of you." She sounded more resigned than angry. "Not that half the world doesn't know. In any case you make no secret of your affairs. I don't understand you. And God knows why I have to continue staying here."

Diana could imagine her tall, handsome master smiling in that special way. He had the appealing way that made everyone love him so much. The smile was in his voice, coaxing his wife out of her bad mood.

"Darling, you do understand. This woman means nothing to me. More than ever has. It's simply a gentleman's pass time, like darts or scrabble. My father did the same thing. So did his father. And so does every sophisticated man. It makes us better husbands; this kind of harmless diversion: More appreciative of women of our own class. Less educated and illiterate women understand this perfectly. I don't know why you highly educated women find it so hard to accept.

"Not hard, Henry. Impossible."

He sounded genuinely amazed. "But why Ann? It's so unimportant. I am your husband. I adore you. I give you everything. You're much too wise to be troubled by the few amusing hours I spend elsewhere. If I drunk heavily or gambled away our money or abused you in any way, you would have a reason to be unhappy, but…"

"You do abuse me. You demean me. You destroy my ego."

He began to sound angry. "What Freudian nonsense is that? You have a beautiful mansion, expensive clothes and jewels, trips to Mombasa and Masai Mara whenever you want to. You have security, social position, and a husband who's proud of you. What more could any woman want?"

"Fidelity, perhaps."

"Fidelity? I think you are using the wrong word. You have fidelity. I am faithful to you and our life in all the ways that count. No my dear, you mean Christian monogamy. That's what you think you want; One woman for one man for all the time. My visits to some feather-brained creature are no more significant to me than an evening at the theatre. They keep me from becoming dull and stodgy. Is that what you would like me to be, my love? A pure but boring husband, I really doubt it."

Diana could hear choked back tears in Ann's voice. "Am I dull and stodgy because I am faithful to you Henry? Is it different for women? How would you feel if you knew I was with another man, even if he meant nothing to me? Wouldn't you feel that you weren't man enough? That somehow you are inadequate?"

There was ghostly silence, and then, Henry said gently, "Dearest, you're being ridiculous. You are a lady. There's no comparison between the physical urges of sexes. We've been over this a hundred times. In all our life together, I have been totally honest with you. I haven't given you any the less of me. Why start this again, just because of that ill-advised call? I told you I am sorry about it, but it isn't as though you didn't know she existed. You know about everyone. But because they are no threat to you, darling, I wouldn't insult you by sneaking around corners. I respect you. You're my wife."

There was long silence before Ann said, "It's useless to talk about this any more. Just remember one thing, Henry. I know these women are in your life. I have been spineless enough to accept and ignore it, but from now on, never allow any of them to approach me; in person or by phone. I swear to you, if they do, I won't be responsible for my actions.

Diana waited a few more minutes, but no further words were spoken. When she entered with a tray of coffee, they were sitting in their usual chairs. If she hadn't overheard their quarrel, she would have assumed it was an evening like any other. But it wasn't. They were angry with each other, and she wished she could help.

*Captive of Fate*

# CHAPTER TWENTY SIX

It was around 2.00 am in the morning. Ann had just dozed off after a sleepless night. She was feeling unwell throughout the day but her efforts to trace Henry in the office had been in vain. Suddenly, she was awoken by Henry's wild knocks and yelling, as he demanded for her to open the door.

She wasn't amused at the behaviour. She knew that he had keys to both the gate and the house. Why he had decided to misbehave is something she couldn't understand. What was going on with Henry? He seemed to be getting worse. How was she going to cope during the remaining months before her delivery? This was becoming absurd.

Full of furry, she jumped out of bed ignoring her painful back. One thing she was sure of was that in his state, if she ignored him, he would wake up everyone in the Estate. "What an embarrassment!" she thought as she went to open the door. "Dear God! I have a husband and a half. Coming home at two o'clock in the morning! Wherever the beast is coming from, I wish he was reasonable enough to spend the night there." She grumbled to herself remembering the number of times she had phoned his office during the day in vain. Every time the phone rung, it was picked by a woman whose response was automatic, "Henry is out. Any message please?" She felt angry with him now. They had to sort out things there and then. She felt she had been bending too low. She switched on the lights to search for the keys so that she could open the door.

"You woman! Open the door quickly. Who are you talking to inside there? Didn't you hear me hoot? Must I alight and knock. You ungrateful rat. Open the door or I will break it."

Ann felt disgusted. "Ungrateful rat!" Damn him! She was going to prove that she was one. Choked with fury, she unlocked the door and stood aside while Henry burst in looking haggard with a bottle of Whisky in his left hand. Stepping behind him to lock the door, she leaned on it and looked at him with such disgust in her eyes that he felt provoked to react.

"What sort of woman are you? You take centuries to open the door and then you stand there looking at me as if I was stinking of human shit instead of giving me food. What the hell is going on in this house? And by the way who were you talking to while you kept me waiting at the door?" He demanded moving towards her with every intention of slapping her.

Instead of moving away from his advance, she stood firm and looked at him calmly. "Nothing is happening here except for your sickening yells." She felt anger beginning to rise and she couldn't withhold it any longer. "Is this the type of life you meant when you promised that you would make my life happy when you wanted to marry me? Didn't you promise to love and care for me Henry, why do you make my life so miserable?" The words came out as if they were choking her. Tears flowed uncontrollably as she struggled to keep herself steady on her feet. She had decided to face him and she wasn't going to let her fury betray her. Wiping the tears with the back of her hand, she prayed silently that her courage should not let her down.

Henry didn't advance further. He seemed perplexed. He had expected to find a scared chicken but she was turning out to be a lioness.

"I wonder if your mother ever taught you how to behave in the presence of your husband. I regret having married a woman whose background I barely knew." He roared staring at Ann who stood calmly looking at him as if she didn't care what he did anymore.

Ann felt hurt by his remarks but she wasn't going to give up. So he was aware that their marriage was a mistake, she thought bitterly. If only she had been a bit careful to avoid getting pregnant so soon, may be things would be different. These thoughts disturbed her mind but she had to brush them aside. She had to tell him her piece of mind too if he thought she was ignorant about the topic.

"Huh! If your mother ever taught you how to behave!" she repeated his statement sarcastically. "And you! Did your father ever teach you how to behave in marriage? Where are you from at this unholy hour? I am sorry to tell you this but I can't help it. Find yourself another wife who will cope with your lousy behaviour. I am not your slave. I am your wife." Ignoring his disgusted look, she moved on to the nearby seat and sat down.

"Ann!" Henry sounded calmer and sober. "You should know that I am your husband and traditionally you are bound to obey me at all times. Don't think that your useless degree and the baseless feminist philosophies of equality which you gathered at the University will make you rule over me here. That one you have to get it out of your imagination. Look here Ann," he began to pace the room quietly as if disturbed beyond what he could bear and then turning to Ann, he decided to pump some sense into her concerning his view of feminism. He looked serious and Ann knew he was sobering up and loved it. All she needed was time to gather more ideas to sober him out completely.

"Ann!" he stood facing her. "The women's liberation warriors think that they have something new but it's just another army coming out of the hills. Bright women ambush men at their cradles in the bedroom and their perfect work in the kitchen. This issue of women's rights is bullshit." He paused and waited for her comment but when he realised that she wasn't going to, he went on.

"Women's liberators think that men have power and control over their lives. It's bullshit about the fraction of a percentage of men who have this power. Ann, those guys aren't men. They aren't even human. That's whose place women have to take. They don't even know that you have to kill to get up there. Thus, what these women aspire to get is what men have; which is shit and heart-aches." He spat on the floor and proceeded, "Plus other shitty jobs men hate to do. Do you understand sweet wife?"

"No. You misinterpret feminists. That's your own presumption. It isn't true. Our..."

"Bullshit", he interrupted before she could conclude her statement.

"The truth is this Ann, in the old days, women didn't know that they had the so-called women's rights and they did a perfect job in their marriages as defined by society. But now that you know, you don't want to be fired no matter how lousy your work is; lousy in bed, lousy in the kitchen and lousy everywhere. You can name it." The last words were screamed rather than spoken. Moved with furry he held her shoulders and shook her to drive his point home. "Listen Ann, it's traditional that you learn to behave like a woman in my presence. I am not going to live with another man in the name of a wife who defies my orders. Do you understand?"

"Keep your filthy hands off me you devil." Ann shook him off and stood up to face him.

"You would better forget about tradition now. I am not going to let you use tradition to torture me. We are living in a different generation, with a different tradition far much different from your fifteenth century one." She was happy that he had turned that topic intellectual and she determined to challenge him intellectually. "Let me tell you the truth Henry. If you want me behave like your grandmother, you will have to behave like your grandfather too."

"Look here Ann!" he interrupted, "I didn't tell you to put on a hide like our grandmothers did. Don't misinterpret me. All I want is your respect as my wife. Don't forget that you're a Christian too and the Christian teachings stress this fact."

"Forget it." Ann snapped. "I don't even understand you Henry. I don't see the reason why men think we should select only what suits them from tradition and religion and discard other important issues. That's unfair. Infact, from your perception of feminism, I can see so many inconsistencies. Your concept is biased and patriarchal. Let me tell you that your traditional conviction about the place of a woman in society is fascist in reality. This is a philosophy that reduces women to mere objects of leisure and amusement for men." She looked at him and realising that he was interested, she resolved to go on.

Henry moved and sat on the nearby seat. "Go on" he said encouragingly amazed by her reasoning. She proceeded without hesitation.

"Women are potrayed as if they have nothing else to do but to manipulate men both in body and soul. God forbid. When the women take part in political issues, they are seen as destroyers of men striving to better the world. Even film producers, musicians and writers have never drawn a relationship between men and women in which sex does not play a major role. Why? Can't they even show, just at one goddamn time that women have other virtues of humanity and unwavering urge to go forward?" She paused expecting him to react but when he kept quiet she went on. "This carried on tradition doesn't seem to have the imagination to foresee that women might just love to be portrayed as real human beings rather than puppets that can't break strings men attach to them? I think that gives you the reason, why women liberators had to emerge from their guerrilla hills to liberate the suffering tradition bound women from their graves of misery by teaching them to learn to ask why? And how? Indeed, it's for this reason that I stand to claim my rights. If anything, you should stop appealing to religious convictions as a weapon to oppress me. As far as I know, the Christian concept of marriage is Hebraic in totality. It is male chauvinistic in the nature of what constitute loveable women. Infact what is defined as a loveable woman in proverbs chapter twelve confirms my perception of a woman as a bondage slave. But anyway, I think the best thing to do in this marriage is to compromise as a couple. Thus, if you expect me to behave traditionally, you'll have to go traditional too.

"Whatever you mean?" Henry said.

"Yes, what I know is that our grandfathers behaved responsibly. They never returned home after midnight, drunk and yelling for food without enquiring about their pregnant wives' status. Try to be responsible Henry," she pleaded.

"Ann! Are you abusing me?" Henry asked angrily. "Do you mean that I am irresponsible?"

"Somehow. Because you don't know how I am feeling now and you don't care. I have been sick since yesterday. I tried to ring your office several times but you were nowhere. And then, you come home at 2 o'clock drunk and yelling for food. What a husband?"

"I said, stop insulting me Ann. Shut up that beak or I will shut it up for you," Henry rose in fury. "After spending every penny I get to make you comfortable, you can shamelessly pour that filthy scorn on me. You ungrateful rat, you are a bitch." He slapped her hard on the face hoping it would end the argument but it didn't. Ann was prepared to fight on.

"I didn't marry you for your money or wealth." She replied flimsily, trying to suppress her fury. "I can as well peddle myself to get money or material things without being tied to a beast of a man in the name of a husband. Marriage means more than that Henry." She tried to calm down. "It has nothing to do with dressing, or eating well. It incorporates soul and body. Why don't you care about my feelings? Have you lost your taste for me? Tell me. I will walk out of here and leave you in peace. It's you I want in this house. Forget about every form of comfort you think you have provided."

"Shut up, you harlot." He screamed it rather than spoke.

"Sure, you can call me that because I am under your roof. I don't object. But what I know is that, where there's a female harlot, there lies a male harlot. May be you are worse than all because you don't even respect your office. Who doesn't know that you sleep with women unselectively in your office? In fact all women who qualify for the advertisement business have to pass the romance test. I think you are a sadist." Ann felt she was getting too far than she had anticipated but she couldn't stop. The words were following involuntarily.

Insulted beyond what he could bear, Henry had to react. "Look here Ann." Like any other man the only weapon remaining was to use force. "Are you going mad?"

"Possibly. And if I do, it's because you drove me into it. I don't care…"

"Shut up your filthy mouth. Shameless whore. How many times have I called this house and missed you? As my wife I don't expect you to leave this house without my knowledge. What itches you? All you can do is move from here and there picking unnecessary gossip. Is it cancer of the rectum you have that makes it uncomfortable to sit in this house? Tell me, you shameless pig?" He shook her violently until she felt pain in her tummy and groaned.

Shaking him off she gasped, "What?" she then stood and moved away from him before turning round to respond to his statement. "Cancer of the rectum! Are you crazy? If I have cancer of the rectum, then you have haemorrhoids, and on a day to day basis, which is far much irritating. You hardly spend time in this house if not in the office. What do you expect me to do when you can't even allow me to get a job to keep me busy? Just sit around and watch your property? No. I am not a watchman. If you need one, get him or her from Opiss Kenya."

Henry felt pushed too far. Overcame by fury, he began to shake. And then as if he had lost his mind, he moved and struck her hard on the face. Realising that she wasn't responding to it, he threw a kick at her stomach without considering her state. He realised his mistake too late. Regrets wouldn't help.

The kick sent Ann flying across the table. She landed on the wall opposite and knocked her head on the wall so hard that she lost consciousness. "I told you that if you didn't shut up your mouth, I would do it for you. Yes, you asked for it." He was so much angry that he didn't care anymore. But suddenly he came back to his senses and sobered. He realised that Ann was not moving and when he moved near to turn her over, he found her still, bleeding profusely from the nose. At first, he was shocked and almost lost consciousness too. But he tried to be strong. He had to act fast.

"God help me. Don't let her lose the baby." He muttered as he bent over and tried to make her lie on her back with his trembling hands. "Ann! Ann dear!" She didn't respond. "I am sorry. I didn't mean to…" he stopped abruptly and put his right ear on her chest to

feel her heartbeat. It wasn't beating normally but it was at least
there. "Oh God, don't let her die." As he spoke this, he lifted her up
to the bedroom and laid her on the bed. For the first time, he felt
confused. He didn't know what step to take, but when he saw the
increase of blood oozing from her nose, he became alert. Picking a
towel from the wardrobe, he ran to wet it in the bathoom and then
placed it around her forehead before rushing to call for an ambulance.

Voices came and went, murmuring unitenlligible phrases. Cool
hands administered to her from time to time but nothing registered
until her friend; Faith's clear voice penetrated the thick layer of fog
that had encased her mind. Henry had called Faith as soon as his
wife got admitted at Kenyatta Hospital.

"Ann?" Her familiar hand gripped hers tightly. "How do you
feel now?"

"I...I have a terrible headache" she complained weakly,
confused by the realisation that she was lying in bed and perturbed
by the excruciating pain in her head when she tried to raise it.
"What...What happened?"

"I think you had a fracas with Henry which ended up in an
accident."

"Oh, yes. I remember now" the memory of that electric slap
flashed through her brain like a nightmare and then a more pressing
thought came to her mind, making her clutch urgently at Faith's
hand as fear consumed her.

"My baby...What happened to it?" She felt searing pain in
her tummy and felt miserable.

"I am sorry." Faith replied finding it difficult to explain but a
nurse standing near by stepped in to explain.

"Indeed we're very sorry. We tried our best to save his life,
but he...he died. However you don't have to worry. Your life is
more important. You can always have another one when you
recover." The nurse explained while Faith looked on.

"Oh God," she croaked, unable to check the tears that filled her eyes but then, she remembered Henry's arrogance and sighed. "This marks the end of my misery under his roof." She thought silently. It took sometime before she spoke. The nurse had left.

"Faith, will you call Grace and inform her that I won't be able to see her this morning she asked?" There was an awkward silence, and then, Faith said cautiously, "Ann, it is evening."

"Evening?" Her mind groped wildly for understanding, but it evaded her. "You have been unconscious since early this morning." "Faith explained in a shaky voice.

"Oh Lord" she moaned. "Was it as bad as that?"

"You were extremely fortunate." Faith explained with relief. You bashed the side of your head badly when you fell, but you have no other injuries except for a few, nasty bruises and the miscarriage."

Ann fingered the starched sheets and asked warily, "Am I in hospital?" Faith was amused by her confusion and replied, "Yes."

Just then, a nurse entered the ward to announce that it was time for Faith to leave. She stood up at once and leaned over Ann to kiss her on the cheek. "I will see you again tomorrow morning." She whispered. Ann then found herself alone with a silent but efficient nurse who took her pulse and her temperature and checked the dressing on her tummy where the pain continued to throb. The nurse then gave her two tablets to take with some water before she told her, "He's been waiting very anxiously since morning to have a word with you."

"Who?" Ann asked hesitantly, and felt odd tension gripping her.

"Your husband."

"My husband?" she repeated with anguish, then her control seemed to snap. As if she were from some distance away, she heard herself crying out in a near-hysterical voice.

"No! Oh, No! Send him away! I don't want to see him. Send him away."

Please wait outside Mr. Odibo, an authoritative voice instructed, as Ann clutched wildly at the arms that held her down.

"Send him way. Don't let him in here please, I don't want…"
"Sister, quick!" she heard male a voice command. A shutter seemed to click in her brain and then, a black- out.

# CHAPTER TWENTY SEVEN

Ann! Ann please wake up and talk to me." Faith's sharp voice struck her consciousness faintly. She had been asleep for over twelve hours following the heavy sedation the previous evening.Worried of her state, Faith had taken leave from work to stay by her side and monitor her progress but for all the time she stayed there, Ann didn't seem to show any sign of waking up.

"Ann!" She kissed her cheek and squeezed her palm. Ann opened her eyes and closed them again as if she hadn't seen her.

"Ann! Don't go back to sleep again." Faith pleaded. In her restored consciousness Ann recognised the familiar voice but felt too weak to respond. She didn't even wish to open her eyes because the light was too bright for her weak eyes.

As she recalled the previous day's incidences, eddying darkness swarm round her and reflection came in as black and confusing as a flow. In this state she sunk into a dream where she saw herself laid down in a dry bed of a great river and floods loosened in remote torrents. As the waters came, she had no will to rise or strength to flee. She just lay there faint, longing for death. One idea only still throbbed life within her; a remembrance of God's protection. It begot an unuttered prayer with the following words wandering up and down in her ragless mind as something that should be whispered but no strength was found to express them.

"In the midst of trouble, God will preserve my life. He's an ever present help at the time of trouble."

Indeed, trouble had overwhelmed her and since she had not lifted the petition to heaven to avert it or joined hands or knelt down or moved her lips to pray, it had come. In full swing the torrent poured over her.

Ann wrestled with the desire for rescue. She wanted to be weak that she might die and avoid the awful passage of further suffering. Conscience turned tyrant and held passion by the throat telling her tauntly that she had dipped her dirty foot in the slough and swore that with that arm, it would thrust her down to unsound depth of agony.

"Let me be torn away. Someone help me!" she cried in the nightmare.

"No. You shall tear yourself away. None shall help you. You shall pluck out your right eye yourself, cut off your right hand and remain the victim and the priest to transfix it." She rose suddenly struck by terror.

"What shall I do?" Her head swarm, as she sat up.

"I am here Ann. Don't worry. I will take care of you." Faith said as she jumped to pin her back on the bed, afraid that she was still having nightmares. No food had passed through her lips and she looked sickeningly pale.

"Can I give you something to eat? You should be hungry."

"No. Don't bother Faith. Let me die."

"But why Ann? I am here for you. I will do everything." Faith pleaded, and realising that she was calm, she moved away to pour some juice for her.

Three weeks had passed since Faith discharged her from hospital and took her to her house when she refused to return to Henry's house. Although she felt strong, Faith had insisted that she stays in bed until she completed the one-month bed rest recommended by the doctor.

With all the attention Faith struggled to offer, Ann still felt miserable. In her perception, she didn't deserve it and wondered why her friend had sacrificed so much to save her life when she deserved to die. She had driven herself into the mess and had to find her way out. "But how?" This question kept recurring in her mind.

It was a hot afternoon and Faith was still at work. As she lay in bed, she began to reflect on her life. The thought of a whole fabric of her life torn, her love lost and her hopes dashed strangled every wish to live. Deep in her thought Ann wondered. She who had been once an ardent, expectant woman, almost successful in life had turned back into a cold solitary girl again. Her life was pale and her prospects desolate. Her hopes were all dead, struck with a subtle doom she could barely interpret. She looked on her cherished wishes of yesterday, so blooming and glowing, but now they lay stark; chilly, livid corpses that could never be revived. This feeling of hopelessness was unbearable and she had to do something. "What shall I do?" She said loudly, hot tears pushing their way out of her eyes. The first answer came in her mind; "Leave Nairobi at once. But to where?" She wondered. Then another came; "Commit suicide. All you need is a packet of Maladrin talets."

These words were prompt, so dread that she closed her ears. She thought she could not bear such a decision. Of what benefit could it be? Or whose? It would be an easy way out of the indefinite fate but what about those who cared for her and cherished her existence like Faith and her parents?"

"Ann! I am home!" Faith's presence in the house intercepted her thoughts. She had to pull herself together for her friend's sake.

"Hey, welcome back." She wiped her eyes and jumped out of bed to meet Faith who was already at the door.

"How are you Ann. You look ill". Faith said hugging her. "Your face is pale. Have you been crying?" she added after a short while.

"I am sorry Faith. I just can't stop feeling sorry for myself."

"Well, you don't have to because God loves you. And He wants to heal your mixed past if only you could give Him the chance. Remember how far He has brought you. And furthermore, you have me." Faith said encouragingly. "I will do everything to see you up on your feet again.

"But you have already done more than you ought to. I don't want to burden you Faith. I have to pick up the pieces of my life and…"

"You don't have to." Faith interrupted. "Here, I made an application on your behalf to one of the Banking Corporations following an advert in the newspaper and here is your invitation for interview. I wish you the best of luck Ann." She said hugging her. "I have also talked to a friend who is one of the senior managers at the Head Office. I think everything will go well."

"Thank you Faith. I don't know what to say. How can I repay your kindness to me? I mean…"

"It's okay Ann. It's my pleasure. Why can't you get into something decent? I am taking you out for dinner.

"Wow! You are full of surprises." She exclaimed standing to leave.

"Oh. This isn't my arrangement. It's Grace and Eshol's. Mary and Jesse are coming too."

"That's great. It's the most wonderful thing that has ever happened to me since I left Campus."

# CHAPTER TWENTY EIGHT

I don't think I am the right girl for you. You deserve a decent woman Henry. I am getting convinced that this relationship was not meant to be. It was a big mistake." Mercy tried to structure her words carefully to avoid hurting Henry.

After his break up with Ann, Henry had virtually moved in with Mercy. She loved his money and all other favours she enjoyed as his mistress but she was feeling trapped. She had to break loose before it was too late.

"What do you mean?" Henry asked perturbed by the unexpected turn of events. When reality struck that he had lost Ann for good, he resolved to settle with Mercy. For close to three months, their relationship seemed perfect. Being a fun type chick, they spent nearly every free time he had together, loving each other and making out as much as time allowed them to. She was a great girl but unpredictable. He was determined to mould her into the kind of woman he wanted for a wife to suit his status.

"What I mean is that this relationship has to end now. It has no future as far as I am concerned. I don't want to waste your time any more."

"But dear, I had all hopes that ..." Henry hesitated looking for the right words.

"But what? I made it clear right from the beginning that marriage is not possible between us. Think about the age gap between us. I have dreams to pursue and you are not one of them. Please understand."

Henry realised that pursuing the subject further was hopeless. He excused himself from the painful conversation and left.

"Women!" Henry cursed as he drove off to his house. "What do women want from men to be content?" He said bitterly recalling his marriage break up with Ann because of his obsession with Mercy and the eventual rejection.

As he sat on the couch in his lounge sipping his favourite beer, Henry felt miserable. With his financial and social status, it would have seemed natural for women to fight for his attention. But his case was a complete reverse. Being rejected by a gold digger like Mercy was humiliating. Enlightened by her shameless rejection he realised how wrong he was to break up his family for her attention.

"May be I should forget about marriage and relationships for a while and enjoy life without stress." Henry thought. He had not been to his favourite Casino for over three months. It was time to make up with his old friends, he resolved.

For about six months Henry enjoyed his carefree lifestyle drinking and exchanging women at will. He did not stop at any time to think of the implications of his immoral behaviour until Sophie intervened.

When Sophie returned from Australia after her postgraduate studies, Sophie realised that her cousin had changed drastically. Besides his heavy drinking habit, he brought home different women frequently with complete disregard to his cousin's discomfort. She resolved to find out from his close friends what was really happening with Henry. The revelations she got were devastating. She was informed that the women Henry brought home were not ordinary girlfriends but hookers from the notorious Koinange Street. Disappointed by the findings she resolved to confront him.

Henry dismissed Sophie's concerns over his lifestyle as unnecessary and unjustifiable. He emphasized that he was an adult and fully responsible for his actions. After several attempts to make him understand the consequences of his actions Sophie gave up and resolved to let him learn through experience.

When Henry called his doctor to book a medical appointment for a routine check up, he did not expect negative results because basically he felt fine except for the noted weight loss that he attributed to the persistent flu attacks and loss of appetite. He was perplexed when the doctor requested him to consider an HIV test.

"Is it really necessary?" Henry asked upset by the doctor's suggestion.

"Yes. It is very important for you to know your status. It will help you to make right decisions concerning your life." The doctor explained in detail the merits of taking HIV tests at leased after every six months as long as he was sexually active outside marriage. Convinced by the doctor's counsel, Henry agreed to undertake the recommended HIV test and requested the doctor to forward the results to him at his office.

When the doctor called him and advised him to collect the results personally, Henry sensed that something was a miss. Normally, the doctor would inform him of his health status on phone or ask him to send someone to collect his prescription for simple ailments like common colds.

As he drove to the doctor's clinic for the results, Henry wondered how he should react if the HIV test results turned out positive. Would he really accept the status and live positively as advised by the doctor? Was that kind of life worth living? "No it can't happen to me." He protested.

Henry thought about some of his friends and employees who had died from Aids and those who were living with HIV and froze with fear. The car from the opposite direction hooted impatiently bringing him back to his senses. He realised that he was actually driving on the wrong lane. He swerved quickly to avoid a head on collision.

"Oh God! What is happening to me?" He exclaimed and resolved to concentrate on the traffic.

When the doctor handed him the results after a long counsel on managing HIV status, Henry felt indifferent. Tormented by the turn of events, he could not tell immediately what option he would consider under the prevailing circumstances. He needed time to think it over properly.

It was around 3.30 in the afternoon when he left the doctor's office. Instead of going back to the office, he drove off to the club to drink off his frustrations. On the way to the club he called Sophie and asked her to meet him at the club after work. He also requested her to contact his lawyer and schedule a meeting later in the evening at the club.

Sophie found it unusual for Henry to make such abrupt arrangements without a serious cause. She resolved to comply out of curiosity. Convincing herself that her cousin was in some serious trouble, she called the lawyer and made necessary arrangement as required before leaving the office.

As she drove off to the club, Sophie received a call on her mobile phone from an unknown caller. She ignored the caller for a while but the call persisted prompting her to switch off the phone because she was driving.

At the club's parking yard, she switched on the phone to call Henry and confirm his location at the club. To her surprise the voice that responded was female and the news she received was devastating. She was informed that Henry had been involved in a tragic road accident at Uhuru Highway a few hours after he called her and died on the way to Kenyatta national hospital. She was required to report to central police station for more information.

# CHAPTER TWENTY NINE

Two months had passed since she got the job at African Finance Corporation as a management trainee, based at the Eldoret Branch. She had assured herself that after what had happened with Henry and with a job, she wouldn't think of getting involved with a man again. But this wasn't the case. The coloured memories of the past began to brighten up into her again and once in a while she thought of Kombo and their painful parting.

After what happened in her marriage to Henry, she began to feel that her judgement of Kombo had been too harsh and wished she could trace him and apologise. After a few weeks of debating about it, she resolved to call one of her favourite lecturers at K.I.U to establish his whereabouts. She also hoped to find him in the office since they shared the same office.

"Hallo" Ann waited patiently.

"My name is Ann Maloba. I..." Before she could finish the introduction, Dr. Ayot interjected.

"Oh sweet Ann, where are you? What happened to my bright student in whom I had all hopes to replace me in this department?" She went on for a while explaining to Ann how their efforts to contact her for a master's degree sponsorship failed due to loss of contact and many other things that had happened after she left.

"And what about Kombo?" she asked finally when she got the opportunity after Ayot's unending narratives.

"Oh poor Kombo!" she exclaimed, "I am afraid I don't have good news about him."

"What happened?" she asked afraid of what Ayot implied in the sentiment.

Dr. Ayot hesitated as if looking for the right words to explain the reality. "Actually, he is no longer with us." She finally let out the truth.

"Oh No. Don't tell me that he's dead."
An remarked impulsively.

"Don't jump to conclusions Ann," she cautioned her before proceeding to explain how Kombo was trapped in a love spell with a student who later dumped him and that unable to endure, he had succumbed to the hand of fate.

"What do you mean doctor? Please tell me exactly what happened." Ann pleaded, guilty of the awareness that she could be the cause.

"Why all the curious interest Ann? I hope you aren't the suspect." She teased her before proceeding to explain. "This is what I mean Ann. After the crisis, he could barely concentrate on his work. I don't blame him. Love is poison." She paused before continuing. "You know, if you handle it carelessly, you may even die."

"Get to the point doctor. We could be disconnected before I get the right information." She interrupted.

"Okay, He tried chasing her to restore the relationship but didn't succeed."

"And then?" Ann asked.

"And then what Ann? He went crazy."

"How?" she demanded.

"At first, he locked himself in his house and could only get out of the house at night when he walked about the streets as if he was out of his senses. As you know, he had been a keener bold man before this fate struck but afterwards, I don't think I have the right words to express."

"What do you mean exactly?"

"What I mean is simple. Initially, He was not a man given to drinking or a reckless living as he turned out to be. If he came to work at all, he would lock himself in the office and cry like an orphaned child. Unable to contain his behaviour, the Management had to dismiss him from service."

"Oh No!" Ann exclaimed. "Do you have any idea of what happened to him after the dismissal?"

"Yes" Ayot confirmed. "He was taken to Mathare hospital for the mentally ill where he stayed for a while. When he came out, he was more confused than when he went in."

"Meaning!" Ann persisted.

"What I mean is that he dropped his profession and became a preacher. I hear that he is a pastor of a church in Eldoret."

"Eldoret? Which Church?" she asked excited by the coincidence of their station.

"EE... Revival Christian Centre. I think it is stationed at Outer Ring Estate. So far, this is the much I can tell you, about Kombo. If you may excuse me, I have a class in five minutes time. Bye." The phone clicked on her side as Ann sat dumbfounded by her findings.

On her way back home from office Ann thought seriously about Kombo's misfortune. She felt responsible for his untold suffering and wished she could turn back the time to erase the misunderstanding that had cost them so much pain in life. When she went to bed that evening she prayed to God for forgiveness and asked Him to bless Kombo and fulfil his lost dreams in life.

The room was full of moonlight that penetrated through the half-drawn curtains. It was hot and she preferred leaving the windows open because the bedroom was upstairs. The environment was quiet but she could not sleep. She was still disturbed by her conversation with Dr. Ayot and as images of what Kombo went through rehearsed in her mind, the urge to reach him became irresistible. Her heart beat first. Infact she could hear its throbs but suddenly it stopped to an inexpressible feeling that, thrilled through and passed at once to her head and its extremities. The feeling wasn't like an electric shock but it was quite sharp, strange and startling. It activated her senses as if their utmost activity hitherto had been but torpor from which they were now summoned and forced to work. She rose expectant, eye and ear waiting, while the flesh quivered on her bones.

Unconsciously she jumped out of bed and switched on the lights. The brightness in the room scared her. She had heard a familiar voice calling from somewhere in the house. It was Kombo's she couldn't doubt it. It was calling her name, "Ann! Ann!"

"Oh God! What is it?" she gasped. The most frightening thing was the where-about of the voice. Where was if from? It didn't seem to have come from the house and neither did it appear to have come from outside, under the earth or over head. But the fact was that she heard it and it was the voice of someone she knew and once loved. It had spoken in pain and woe wildly, eerily and urgently. "I should be hallucinating," She thought, but how could it be so real? She wondered.

Unconsciously she proceeded to respond to the voice and ran down the stairs. "I am coming." She stopped halfway and peered through the dark passage. It was dark and void. Overwhelmed with frustration and fear, she broke into sobs and ran back to her room where she knelt down and started praying.

# CHAPTER THIRTY

Ann didn't have to ask to find the location of Revival Christian Centre. After leaving office at 5 o'clock the next evening, she resolved to take the bus to Outer Ring estate to try and confirm Dr. Ayot's allegations. It was hard to believe that God could change a wreckless wretch like Kombo into a powerful servant. She had heard about the performance of his church and if he was indeed its pastor, then she would confirm the belief that everything is possible with God.

She alighted from the bus at 6.45 following a delay in boarding the bus due to long queues. As she stood outside the church's gate, she wondered if Kombo was still single. "What if he was married? How was he going to react to her resurface? "God give me the grace to handle this situation diligently." She prayed as the watchman opened the gate and greeted her.

"I am looking for Mr. Kombo. Is he the pastor here and where does he stay?" She asked after responding to his greetings. "Oh yes. You are in the right place. He stays in that house. Infact, he is the one standing outside." The watchman replied in Kiswahili.

As she walked towards the building, Ann saw the image standing under a tree. It brought back the memories of the past making her feel weak. Images of her past experiences with him passed in her mind like a film on a projector. Her head ached and she wished she could lie down and rest. The figure under the tree hadn't noticed her advance yet. But it was Kombo; that she couldn't doubt. He had changed so much. He had grown slender and had a huge beard. Adjusting her steps and breath, she stood to examine him, while she remained unseen to him. It was a sudden meeting and one in which rapture was kept well in check by uncertainty.

Examining him carefully she realised that his form was of the same strong and stalwart contour as ever. His posture was still erect and his hair black. Neither of his features were altered or sunk but in his countenance she saw a change that looked desperate and brooding. This reminded her of some wronged and faltered wild beast or bird, dangerous to approach in its sullen woe. However, Ann didn't fear. A soft hope blended with her sorrow daring her to drop a kiss on that brow and the lips hidden beneath the outgrown mane, but she couldn't. She knew he was a changed man; no longer passionate as she knew him but a mighty and honourable man of God.

Kombo stood with folded arms, quietly leaning on a mango tree and seemed to be in his own world. He however looked lonely and miserable. The distance between them was so short yet he didn't seem to sense her presence. At the moment, Ann gathered all strength and approached him with confidence. Her footsteps on the pavement brought his senses back to the world of the living, as he suddenly became conscious of an intruder.

Assuming that it was one of his church members he turned round and said "Bwana asifiwe!" The words vanished as soon as he recognised who the visitor was, leaving his mouth open and his whole self shocked. He stared at her blankly as if he had seen a ghost.

Ann realised his dilemma and advanced towards him with an apology. "It's me Kombo. Forgive me…"

Inspired by her voice, he recovered immediately from his shock. "Is it really you Ann? I can't…"

"Yes. It is me." She replied without giving him time to complete his sentence.

Without uttering a word, he embraced her. Ann was shocked because she had expected a rejection or even a reproach. "This is impossible." She thought but she was too excited and could not resist the force that drove her to him. They stood in the embrace for a while. During this period, no one spoke. Ann wondered if he was married but dismissed the thought for the time.

For sometime, Kombo remained silent, and then suddenly broke into a thanks-giving prayer. Ann felt confused. She didn't know how to react. Touched by his intercession she broke down and wept. The wetting of his shirt brought him back to consciousness. He had to break the prayer when he realised that she was crying. But if only he could know that those tears were for the joy of their re-union long longed for, he could even have thanked God more.

"This can't be the work of man Ann. It is the divine work of God." He pushed her away and looked at her wet face before embracing her again.

"Oh God! What can I give you to show my gratitude?" Touching her palms he exclaimed; "Her very fingers; slight, small and beautiful. Is it you Ann?" Ann tried to talk but she couldn't. Without waiting for her reply he went on, "But of course yes. Her shape and voice, Oh God! Ann! Ann!"

"Yes dear. It's me and I am grateful to be back with you again. I have come back to you Kombo. Forgive..."Kombo interrupted unable to contain the excitement.

"In truth! In flesh! My living Ann?" he turned her head and looked into her eyes with seriousness as if he would be able to confirm it from there. Ann gathered the strength to talk. She had to explain things right away.

"I left you because I was so jealous. But I was wrong Kombo. I have learnt my lessons and I came to seek your forgiveness."

He recovered from his excitement and asked, "Are you going to stay with me then?"

"Certainly. Unless if you object. I am working and stationed here in Eldoret. I want to be your neighbour, your keeper, your companion and nurse. I don't wish us to be separated ever again."

"Yes Ann. Let nothing separate us again. God is our witness." Kombo said hugging her passionately.